A SEA OF SECRETS AND SALVATION

A MERROWKIN PREQUEL NOVELLA

JENNIFER ALLIS PROVOST

Copyright © 2025 by Jennifer Allis Provost

All rights reserved.

No portion of this book may be reproduced in any form without written permission from the publisher or author, except as permitted by U.S. copyright law.

Cover design by Getcovers Design

CONTENTS

Author's Note	1
1. Stranded	2
2. Rescue	5
3. The Boat	10
4. Chicken is Not a Vegetable	15
5. The Orchard	23
6. Images of Home	29
7. Roasted Potatoes and a Sunset	33
8. Hook, Line, and Sinker	40
9. Hearts Call Out	51
10. Always	56
11. The Morning After	61
12. The City Rises	64
13. Eating, Is It?	69
14. Going Below	74
15. The Feast	77
16. The Most Wonderful Truth	83
17. The King's Blessing	87

18.	The Rest of Their Days	90
19.	Merrowkin Chapter One: The Cliffs	94
Also By Jennifer Allis Provost		104
About The Author		107

AUTHOR'S NOTE

A Sea of Secrets and Salvation takes place approximately twenty-one years before the events in **Merrowkin**. It reveals whether or not a fisherman really did rescue a mermaid stranded beneath the Cliffs of Moher, and what happened afterward. You don't need to have read **Merrowkin** to understand what happens in this story. Aoife and Brian's adventures speak for themselves.

Happy reading!

STRANDED

"This is a fine mess," I grumbled. I kicked a rock, which didn't move but hurt my foot nonetheless. Add that ache to my wounded sword arm, strained throat, and other lingering issues, and I was a sorry excuse for a warrior. "This never would have happened to Scáthach."

I considered Scáthach. Not only was she my elder sister, she was a right terror, and spent her days leading a military academy located off the coast of Scotland. A wise woman would have reached out to her sister for aid, or at least advice, before first arguing with the king, and then plunging headlong into a situation that was larger and more complex than anyone realized. But not me. I'd run off and done things my own way, and now I was wounded and stranded on a beach at the base of the Cliffs of Moher.

Worst of all, I was stranded above.

Furious, mostly with myself, I paced the length of the beach. The two men who'd led me to my unfortunate situation were Gradlon, the monarch of Ker Ys, and a captain of my home city of Kilstiffen's guard called Seamus MacCreehy. Gradlon hadn't been foolish enough to raise his hand to me; no, he had approached me with a treaty of sorts, and while it wasn't anything that physically harmed me, it was a blow nonetheless. And the fact that my father had agreed with Gradlon had hurt further still.

As for Seamus, he was committing nothing short of treason, and I said as much. I'd no sooner drawn my sword when his guards surrounded me. Mindless sycophants, all of them. Even so, those sycophants had effectively kept me from their leader, and one of them landed a lucky blow to my shoulder that rendered my sword arm all but useless. I'd had no choice but to use the magic imbued in my voice to escape the city and then flee upward through the sea, and now my throat was so raw I could barely muster a whisper.

Gods below, I had no idea how I'd get off this beach and back home.

A thrumming sound roused me from my dark thoughts. I looked toward the sea, and saw a white craft on the horizon. The idiot on the boat was back.

"Hello again," the man operating the boat called over. "Have you changed your mind about me coming ashore?"

"Don't you dare come any closer," I screeched, my voice raspier than it usually was thanks to the pain in my throat. "Set foot on this beach and I'll cut off your head!"

"Suit yourself," he said, then he threw two items onto the beach. Assuming they were weapons of a sort, I stood my ground, but kept a sharp eye on the projectiles. Boat Man laughed, and I turned my scowl toward him. He was a young man, with cropped dark hair and a ghost of a beard along his jaw. He'd removed his shirt since he'd last come by to taunt me, and his well-muscled arms and chest were on full display. Boat Man was a handsome idiot, I'd give him that.

"Leave me," I croaked as I flung my arm toward the sea. The movement strained my bad shoulder, and I bit the inside of my mouth to keep from crying out. I'd learned long ago to not show any weakness, physical or otherwise, especially not in front of a *surface dweller*.

Boat Man saw me wince as I held my arm against my body, but he didn't comment on my obvious pain. Instead, he turned the boat around and left, which was all I'd wanted from him. After the craft was out of sight, I approached the missiles he'd lobbed onto the beach. They were two bottles, clear like glass but much lighter, and more pliable. I got one of them open, and found that it contained cool, clean water. I scanned the horizon, and wondered if I'd been too hasty in my treatment of the man. Perhaps he'd spoken the truth, and only wanted to help me. My gaze dropped to the shore, and the sea. It moved closer and closer to my feet as the tides came in.

Perhaps I should have accepted his aid.

Perhaps I should form a real plan, instead of feeling sorry for myself.

I drank more water, which felt like knives against my raw throat. I only needed to allow my throat time to heal, then I would sing and swim my way out of this mess. Soon enough, I would be home, and Seamus would pay for his crimes. As for Gradlon's mad plans, getting around him will take a bit more finesse. Sadly, if there was anything I lacked, it was finesse.

RESCUE

I lay awake all night, thinking about her. The woman on the beach. The way the sunlight had glinted off her pale hair, how her eyes were a bright, clear blue—and the anger flashing in those depths. Add to her obvious beauty her odd clothing and assortment of weaponry, and the lady on the beach was quite the enigma.

I couldn't understand how she'd ended up on that beach, which was nothing more than a thin sliver of land at the base of the near-vertical cliffs. She certainly didn't swim there or climb down from above, and there were no crafts moored nearby. What's more, I asked around at the piers, and no women had been reported missing. It was as if I'd wandered into a fairy tale and met a selkie or siren who'd been waylaid on her journey home... Which would have explained the ethereal singing I'd heard. Following that song was what led me right to the beach, but that woman only screeched and croaked at me. She couldn't have been the one singing such a lovely tune, but if it hadn't been her voice I heard, whose was it?

Magical creatures aside, not only did she need to get off that beach, she was wounded. I recalled how she'd favored her right arm, and the rest of her looked rather beat up as well. Even though she threatened me with a beheading, what she needed was help, and I was going to get her some whether she wanted it or not.

As soon as I got out of bed. I phoned the Coast Guard and gave them her coordinates, then I went down to my boat and headed over to where I'd last seen her. High tide had been at around three in the morning, and for the life of me, I couldn't remember if the beach she was on ever got fully submerged. My gut clenched, and as I steered my craft toward the cliffs, I hoped things hadn't taken a turn for the worse.

When I approached the beach and saw her stalking the length of it like a trapped panther, I breathed a sigh of relief. She was still wearing that odd kit of gold chain mail and leather armour and boots, not that she had luggage with her for a wardrobe change. In fact, aside from her clothing, the only items she had were a round shield strapped to her back, a set of wide gold bracelets on her wrists, and a sword belted at her hip.

I swung the boat around and cut the engine so she could hear me. "I see you survived the night."

"Aye," she replied, but her voice was much weaker than it had been the day prior.

"I've some food and water with me, and I'd like to share it with you," I continued. "Am I allowed to come ashore, or am I still in danger of losing my head?"

She didn't speak, but waved me toward the beach. Taking that as my invitation, I dropped anchor, then I launched the life raft. I'd already stocked it with food, water, a first aid kit, and a few towels. After I'd reached the shore and dragged the raft onto the beach, I offered her a bottle of water.

"It's fresh," I said, when she stared at it as if she'd never seen a plastic bottle before, as if this wasn't identical to the bottles I'd tossed out to her yesterday. I twisted off the cap, and held it out to her. "Want me to drink a bit, and prove to you it's not poisoned?"

She frowned, and shook her head. "Thank you," she rasped, then she drank. "Gods below, thank you for that."

"You're quite welcome. Would you like to sit?" I grabbed one of the towels—the old ratty ones always got demoted to boat duty, a habit I'd learned from my mum—and spread it across the rocky beach. It wouldn't be much of a cushion against the rocks, but at least it was dry. "I've some food, if you're hungry."

"Why are you helping me?" she demanded.

"Because you need help," I replied. "You're obviously stranded out here. I know I'm a stranger to you, but I mean you no harm. If you're willing to get on my boat, I'll take you to the harbor, and then you can be on your way."

"What harbor?" she asked.

"I usually dock at Liscannor, but Doolin's the closest." When her only response was to look toward the sea, I asked, "Is there another harbor you'd like to go to, instead?"

"Doolin? That's the village across from Inisheer?" she asked, naming the closest of the Aran Islands.

"Aye, that's the one."

"They'll find me in Doolin," she murmured. "I need a different place to go ashore, somewhere they won't look for me. I cannot return below before I'm ready."

"Mmm." I had no idea what she meant by that, since the only thing below us was the ocean floor. Instead of pointing that out, I busied myself by sorting through the food I'd brought. Hunger and thirst had been known to drive a person mad. "I brought some energy bars. They taste awful, but if it's calories you're needing, they'll do the job. I've also got some apples, and bread." I tore off a portion of bread and handed it to her. "My name is Brian, by the way. Brian Murphy."

"I'm called Aoife," she replied. "You must think I'm crazy."

"I think you've been stuck on this beach for at least a full day and night, and that's enough to drive anyone off the deep end." I jerked my chin toward the bread. "Go on. Try it."

Aoife accepted the bread and smiled, and damn it all, but that smile went straight to my heart. "It's very good," she said, after she'd had a bite. "Do you live on your boat?"

"It seems that way sometimes, but no," I replied. "I have a house. It's an old farm. Hasn't had a decent crop in years, though I want to start growing again. My dream is to open a restaurant and serve locally grown produce, and seafood caught on my own boat." I paused my rambling, and wondered why I was telling her all of that. I grabbed one of the apples, and offered it to Aoife. "These apples are from my wee orchard."

Aoife took the apple from me, and scrutinized it as if I'd handed her a rare jewel. "App ell," she repeated, stretching out the syllables. "I don't think we have these where I'm from."

Where in the world were apples an oddity? "Are you from far away?"

"It's rather close, actually. How does one eat one of these?"

"I can cut it up for you," I began, then a knife appeared in her hand.

"I can handle slicing it up." She deftly sliced off two portions, and held one out to me. "Have some with me?" I took the piece from her, warily since I still had no idea where that knife came from. "Oh, it's sweet! And crunchy!"

"Have the rest," I said, when she offered me a second slice. She didn't need to be told twice, and I watched as Aoife gobbled down the rest of the apple.

"I see what you're doing, Brian Murphy," Aoife said, as she sliced the last bits of white flesh from the apple's core.

"Oh? What's that, now?"

"You've come onto my beach bearing cool water and exotic treats as your final attempt to get me on that boat of yours," she said, with a sidelong glance at me.

"This is your beach? I was not aware."

"I was here first, so that makes it mine."

"Ah. I stand corrected," I said, as Aoife's smile grew into a full grin. I'd never seen a lovelier sight in all my days. "Has my plan worked?"

"It surely has, and it's been helped along by the fact that I cannot bear to spend another moment on this rocky, soggy bit of sand." She stood, though she still favored her right side. "If your offer still stands, that is."

"Of course it does." I gathered up the few items I'd brought with me and stowed them in the raft, then I faced Aoife. "Before we push off, I need to know how many knives you have on you."

She tensed. "Why is that?"

"The raft's inflatable. A stray poke and we'll be swimming for it."

Aoife tossed back her head and laughed. "Afraid of a dip in the cold water? Fear not, Brian Murphy. Not only do I have excellent control of my blades, I'm a strong swimmer. I won't let you drown."

"Consider me reassured." With that, Aoife got onto the raft, and as I pushed off from the beach, I wondered what I was getting myself into.

THE BOAT

Getting on this man's boat was exactly what I'd sworn not to do, yet here I was. At least I wasn't on that awful strip of beach any longer.

Brian's boat was an interesting craft, stocked with nets and crates and powered by the gadgets surface dwellers favored over magic and the natural way of doing things. Since I had no desire to interact with any of those knobs or handles, I stood to the side while Brian made the necessary adjustments. Once he was done, he turned to me, and frowned.

"I have some dry clothing down in the cabin," he began, as he rubbed the back of his neck. "If you're wanting to lay low, wearing that kit about town isn't the way to do it."

I looked down at myself. Thanks to my time on the beach, my boots were caked in mud, and everything currently in contact with my body was damp and irritating. "Where are these clothes?"

"Follow me," Brian said, and he led me into the cabin. In it was a satchel of various tunics and breeches, all of them made of soft, well-washed fabrics. "The shirts will be a bit big on you, and the trousers have a drawstring for your waist," he explained. "I'll wait up top."

With that, he left me in the cabin with an assortment of clothes... his clothes, I realized. I'd never worn a man's clothes before, and the prospect of putting on Brian's warmed me in a new and not altogether unwelcome fashion. Unwilling to consider exactly how I felt about that, I unbuckled my sword belt and then set it and my shield against the wall, but I gasped when I reached for the fastening on my breastplate. Thanks to my injured shoulder, I couldn't reach the buckles. Swallowing my pride, I went to the door.

"Brian?"

"Aye?"

"I need some help with my armour." When all I heard was silence, I added, "Please."

"Give me a moment," he called. Less than a minute later I heard footsteps, then his large frame filled the cabin's doorway. "What are you needing help with?"

"My breastplate. I need to remove it, but I can't reach the buckles." Brian's brow pinched; no doubt he was wondering why I couldn't perform such a simple motion. "And after the breastplate's off, you'll need to pull the chain mail up and over my head."

"All right, then." Brian unfastened one of the buckles, then he stood behind me and moved my plait to my other shoulder, and undid that buckle as well. "I trust you have something else on underneath your mail?"

"Does it matter? Surely I'm not the first woman you've seen." When he didn't reply, I peeked over my shoulder. Now that we were in close proximity, I realized he was younger than I'd originally thought. Perhaps he was as young as me. Also, his face was as red as that apple he'd fed me earlier.

I paused, feeling a strange mix of apprehension and modesty. Having another—even a man—assist me with my armor was nothing new; I'd grown up in the sparring courts and practice fields along with the rest of the fighters. Bodies weren't new or interesting to me, clothed or not. Brian's hesitation told me that he thought an unclothed body was quite interesting, indeed.

"Am I?" I asked.

Brian grunted, then he lifted both sides of the breastplate away from me. "We'll leave the personal questions for after dinner. Hold still, now." Gently, he gathered up my mail shirt and pulled it over my head. "I never knew mail could be made from gold."

I faced him—I was wearing a loose linen tunic beneath the mail, much to his obvious relief—and said, "Not everyone gets gold mail. And it's only plated; gold is a soft metal, and it wouldn't offer much protection in battle. Iron makes a much better defensive layer."

"Iron. So you're not a fairy?"

I suppressed a smile, but only just. "No. I am not a fairy."

Brian nodded, then he set the mail aside. "What happened to your shoulder?"

"What makes you think anything happened to my shoulder?" I countered.

"For one, you couldn't reach the fastenings on your own breastplate," he said. "For two, you've been favoring your right arm." He scrutinized the right side of my body. "Are those bloodstains, as well?"

"What if they are?"

"If they are, you probably need medical attention," he replied. "Are you so proud you'll stand there in pain instead of accepting help?"

He was right, both about my pride and the battered state of my body. Still, I almost denied admitting any injury, but it had been so long since anyone cared about my wounds in anything beyond a clinical manner. What's more, I did not want any lies between me and this sweet, kind man.

"I found myself among enemies, and one of them drove the hilt of his sword down into me." I moved the neck of my tunic aside, and revealed an angry purple mark right atop the joint. "This injury was why I had to flee, and how I ended up on that beach."

Brian reached for me and paused, his hands hovering over my skin. "May I?"

I nodded. "Yes. Of course."

Brows lowered, he probed my shoulder. His big hands were warm, and gentle. Even so, the pain made me grit my teeth. "It doesn't appear to be broken, but you've a nasty bruise blooming," he said at last. "We should probably wrap it up, and get your arm in a sling. You will, um, need to take this off," he added, as he tugged the edge of my tunic.

This time, I didn't tease him. Instead, I turned my back, and asked, "Give me a hand?"

I felt his firm hands near my waist, then Brian gathered up my tunic and whisked it off my body. He was silent as he set about wrapping my shoulder in a bandage the color of wet sand, then he helped me into one of the shirts he'd offered me earlier. Brian didn't move from his place behind my back, and that was just as well. Every time his hands touched my bare skin my face warmed as my spine shivered, and it was all I could do to keep still. Only when I was properly covered did he speak again.

"That should do, for now," he said. "I've got to check the controls." He exited the room, and closed the door behind him. I set about removing the rest of my clothes and putting on the trews he'd left for me, and joined him on deck.

"So you were in a swordfight," he said when he saw me; he was much more loquacious when I was properly covered. "Was it your first?"

I snorted. "Not hardly."

"Are you a legendary fighter, then? Is that how you earned that fine gold mail?"

"The gold is my birthright."

"Birthright? Is your father a jeweler?"

"I'm the king's daughter." I glanced at Brian, and his handsome, guileless face softened my heart. After the many kindnesses he'd shown me, he deserved nothing less than my full honesty. "My father is the king of Kilstiffen."

"Kilstiffen?" he repeated. "There's a reef out here called Kilstiffen. It's named after a city that…" He took a breath. "Aoife, are you telling me you're from a city that went under the sea centuries ago?"

"I am." I didn't expect him to believe me. Surface dwellers either thought Kilstiffen was nothing more than a myth, or that we'd all perished long ago. The fact that we still existed was much more boring than the dramatic tales of our demise. "I'm hiding up here, because I got in the middle of a plot that might destroy my home. I… I don't know what to do."

Brian set his hand atop mine. "Before we worry about what happens next, let's get to dry land."

CHICKEN IS NOT A VEGETABLE

While I took care of docking the boat, Aoife packed up her armour and weapons in an old knapsack of mine. As soon as we were ready to disembark, I checked the time. It was just before noon. I wondered if the folks down in Kilstiffen were getting ready for lunch.

I glanced at Aoife. She seemed of sound mind, despite that she'd been stranded on that beach for a full day and night, but she claimed she came from a city under the sea. That was ludicrous, and yet...

And yet, I wanted to believe her. It wasn't just because she was pretty, or because I'd enjoyed the few conversations we'd had. There was something about Aoife, an air of confidence that told me she had no need to lie. That meant that she'd told me the truth, or at least what she believed to be the truth. Whether or not it was the actual state of things remained to be seen.

Once we were standing on the harbour walk, Aoife faced me. "I thank you for your aid, Brian Murphy," she said, her back straight as an arrow. "Should you ever find yourself in need while you're out on the sea, call my name. I'll make sure you're safe."

"Thank you," I said. She gave me a curt nod, then she turned on her heel and began walking away from me. My heart clenched, and I knew I couldn't let her go. Not yet, not until I knew more about her. "Aoife!"

She halted, and glanced over her shoulder. "Yes?"

"Have you any place to go?" When she didn't respond, I moved to stand in front of her. "If you'd like, you can come with me. You said yourself you need to recover before you go back and finish that fight. I don't have much, certainly not as much as a king, but I can offer you a safe place to sleep for the night."

"I don't know," she said, shaking her head. "There are people looking for me. I don't want to bring trouble down upon you."

"If they're watching you now, they've already seen me." I held out my hand. She eyed it as if it was a snake reared up to strike. Not only was Aoife a warrior, she wasn't used to people helping her. "If nothing else, you can use my place to catch your breath, and figure out your next move."

"Will you show me your orchard?" she asked. "The one the apples came from?"

"Aye. I will show you the orchard."

"Well then." Aoife took my hand, and every hair on the back of my neck stood up. "It seems that once again I am accepting your offer, Brian Murphy."

God Almighty, the combination of Aoife smiling and holding my hand at the same time was nearly more than I could bear. I shouldered the knapsack that held her things, and we set off toward my home. "Since you're a princess and all, I feel like I should bow," I said. "Maybe do a bit of genuflecting."

"Don't you dare."

We were quiet after that, until we reached my front door. I lived in a farmhouse that had sheltered generations of Murphys, though I was the last one standing. The house was far too big for just me, but it was home nonetheless. Besides, it's not like I had anywhere else to go.

"Here we are," I said, ignoring the dust motes floating in the air. One thing I was not good at was cleaning up. "Would you like to rest for a bit? I've plenty of rooms if you'd like to have a nap."

"Could I trouble you for a bath?" she asked, then she bit her lip. "Forgive me. All I've been doing is troubling you."

"It's no trouble, and of course you can have a bath." I led her into my room. Being that it was the master suite, it had an attached full bathroom, which meant she could have a bit of privacy. I indicated the door off to the side, and said, "The bathroom's just there, and both the shower and tub are at your disposal. Oh, hang on a minute." I ducked out, and retrieved a box of clothes from Donna's room. "Here are some ladies' clothes. They'll probably fit you better than my old things."

Aoife delicately touched the clothes. "Do these belong to your wife?"

"No, because I've no wife," I said in a rush. Why I was in such a rush to reassure Aoife that there was no Mrs Murphy to contend with, I didn't quite know. "These belong to my sister, Donna. She's away at university down in Cork, but I'm sure she wouldn't begrudge sharing a few things with you." I didn't mention that Donna had been gone for almost three years now, or how my parents had moved to Dublin shortly afterward, or how I'd been left behind rattling around this house like the world's loneliest ghost. Aoife had enough of her own problems, and I didn't need to saddle her with mine.

"At any rate, they're all clean," I added. Aoife nodded, and it was then that I noticed how drawn and pale she was. Poor lass was probably exhausted after her ordeal on the beach. "I'll leave you to it. Use whatever you'd like in the bath, and give a yell if you need me. I'll be in the kitchen."

I shut the bedroom door behind me, and went into the kitchen. After I poured myself a glass of water, I sat at the table and held my head in my hands. What in God's name was I doing? This was no mere rescue of a person stranded on a tidal beach. I was inexplicably drawn to Aoife, and not only because I'd helped her out of her armour. Any thrill from her being partially clothed had been overridden by shock when I saw the many wounds on her back and arms, bruises and scrapes and barely healed cuts. I supposed the injuries proved a portion of her story, since she certainly appeared to be a warrior. Whether or not she was a warrior from a city beneath the sea, as well as a king's daughter… Well, the jury was still out on that.

I knew the old stories of Kilstiffen as well as anyone who'd lived their entire life in County Clare. It was a city of such wealth the roofs were made of gold, but somehow all that wealth—and the greed that went along with it—caused the city to sink some time ago. And now there was a woman in my bathroom who claimed to be from that very city. A woman I was going out of my way to keep as close to me as possible.

Who was the mad person here, her or me?

Sitting at the table wasn't going to answer any of my questions, so I turned to what I always did when my mind wouldn't stop racing, and started cooking. Many feel the need to create with their hands and I was no different, but instead of sculpting or painting, I created meals. I'd been serious when I told Aoife about my dream of opening a restaurant, and crafting delicious, hearty fare from produce grown on my own land, and fish caught with my own nets. It was the sole reason why I still lived on the family farm, and why I'd gladly accepted my uncle's tired old fishing rig after he retired to Portugal. I even had my eye on an empty storefront in town; it was the perfect location for a café, or a luncheon spot. I would have to start small, being that I planned on doing all the cooking and baking myself. Perhaps I would only operate during the tourist season for the first few years. Then, if things went well, I could expand.

I wondered if Aoife would like a home cooked meal.

Unsettled at just how easily Aoife slid into my thoughts, I shook my head and took stock of what I'd laid out on the counter. I had a whole chicken, a few lemons, potatoes, carrots, butter, and the rest of that morning's bread. I'd just grabbed my good knife when I heard the bedroom door open. A moment later, Aoife entered the kitchen, and the sight of her stopped me dead in my tracks.

The water had darkened Aoife's blonde hair to a rich golden hue, which somehow made her eyes as blue as sapphires. On her wrists were the gold bracelets she'd been wearing before. Now that they were clean, I noticed they were decorated with blue and green scales. Around her neck was a gold chain with a pearl pendant, simple and elegant. Definitely something a king's daughter would wear.

Aoife had left her hair loose, and put on a strapless white dress that was a stretchy material up top, but loose and flowing from her waist down to her ankles. She'd also removed the bandage from her shoulder, and the large bruise atop her right arm was in full view. Logically, I understood that a strapless dress was probably the easiest thing for her to put on, what with her injured shoulder.

Logic be damned. Aoife in that white dress was the most beautiful sight I had ever seen.

"What's all this?" she asked, tilting her chin toward the food I'd laid out on the counter.

"The makings of our dinner," I replied. "When I need to think, I cook."

She frowned and dropped her gaze. "I suppose I've given you much to consider."

"You certainly have." When she wouldn't meet my eyes, I asked, "Would you like to help with dinner?"

"Certainly." She took a step toward me, and paused. "I think it's fair to warn you that I've never cooked a single thing in my life."

"Yes, I imagine Princess Aoife has an entire staff to see to her many needs."

Her eyes narrowed. "Do you know who calls me Princess Aoife?"

"Everyone?"

"No one who wants to keep their head." She stepped up to the counter and surveyed the vegetables. "What can I do?"

"I know how you like your knives," I said, as I handed her mine. "If you could wash and chop the vegetables, that would be splendid. I'm going to run out back and grab some herbs."

Aoife nodded, and I foolishly thought things were under control. In the time it took me to walk to the greenhouse, pick a handful of thyme and parsley, and re-enter the kitchen, she'd chopped up all the carrots and was cutting into the top of the chicken.

"What are you doing?" I tossed the herbs into the sink and snatched the chicken out from under her. "If you cut up the skin, the meat will dry out in the oven!"

"You said to chop the vegetables!"

"Chicken is not a vegetable." I set the bird down, and wiped my hands on a towel. "What do you eat where you're from? Nothing but fish?"

"We have fish, yes, and things like clams and oysters, and sea vegetables." She poked at a potato. "I've never seen anything like these lumps of dirt."

I blew out a breath, and chose to be calm. "No, I suppose you haven't, living at the bottom of the sea as you do."

She crossed her arms over her chest. "I don't scuttle about the sea floor like a crab!"

"Certainly not. That would be madness." Throwing all caution to the wind, because she still had the knife in her hand and she knew how to use it, I grabbed Aoife about the waist, picked her up, and set her on the counter at the far end of the room.

"How dare you," she began.

"How dare you slice up that poor innocent chicken," I retorted. "Stay here, and I'll finish up." I held out my hand. "My knife, please."

Her lips pressed in a thin line, she set the knife in my palm.

"Thank you." I turned back to the food, and began slicing the potatoes.

"I was only trying to help," she said.

"I realize that," I said. "I should have given you better instructions. Forgive me?"

"We'll see. Is there anything non-food related I can do?"

I finished layering the potatoes in the bottom of the roasting pan, then I grabbed a bottle of wine and a corkscrew. "You can open the wine," I said, as I set them on the table.

Aoife hopped down from the counter, and picked up the corkscrew. "I have no idea what to do with this contraption."

"You're smart. I have faith you'll figure it out." Confident she would be occupied for the next few minutes, I returned my attention to the chicken. I'd just gotten the bird ready to go in the oven, when I heard a crack behind me. I turned, and saw Aoife holding her sword in one hand and the now-open bottle in the other. She'd chopped the top of the bottle's neck clean off without spilling a drop.

"It's open!" she said, her face gleeful.

I was definitely in over my head.

THE ORCHARD

While Brian finished dealing with his precious chicken—which was assuredly not a vegetable—I poured the wine. He had a set of crystal clear heavy glasses, which were quite different from the polished seashells I usually drank from at home. My father would have adored them.

"For you," I said, as I presented him with a glass.

"Is that how they open wine in Kilstiffen?" he asked, as he accepted it. "If you use your swords for that instead of fighting, no wonder someone got the drop on you."

If anyone else had insulted my fighting abilities, their next utterance would be a plea for their life, but the laughter in Brian's eyes calmed my ire. He enjoyed teasing me, and I enjoyed it when he smiled. "If only that were true. Have we some time before the food's ready?"

"A fair bit. Why?"

"You said you would show me your orchard."

"Aye, so I did." He extended his arm to me. I tucked my hand into his elbow, and he led me out of his home and into the most lovely sun filled garden.

"Your home is a paradise," I said. I tilted my face toward the sky, and let the sunlight drench me in warmth. "So much sun, endless sky... Truly, those who live on the surface are the luckiest of all."

"Why don't your people live on the surface?" he asked. "Surely there's enough room up here for everyone."

"My people aren't like yours. We're merrows, and we keep to the tides."

"Merrows. I thought they were half fish," he said, as he glanced at my bare feet.

"Some of us have fish tails, but what we all have is a voice. Our true power is in our songs." I met his gaze, looked away. "When my shoulder was injured, I sang louder and harder than I ever had to get away from them. It's how I ended up on that beach, stranded. I strained my vocal chords so badly I won't be able to sing more than a few croaking notes until they're healed."

"I heard you, out on the water," he said. "Your singing is what first drew me to the beach."

"Did you?" My hands trembled, so I clutched my wineglass with both of them to suppress the shaking. If Brian had been drawn all the way across the sea by my voice... "What was your impression of my song?"

"That it was beautiful, as was the singer." Brian tilted up my chin, and examined my neck. "I can make you some tea with honey, if you like. That should soothe your throat." He glanced at my shoulder. "We should wrap up your shoulder again, too."

"It feels much better after the bath," I said. Brian's fingers lingered on my jaw, then he withdrew his hand and stepped back from me.

That was just as well, since I'd gone hot all the way to my ears. I sipped my wine, which did little to cool me.

"The orchard is just over here," he said, and I followed him toward the far side of the garden. Tucked near a stone wall were three orderly rows of trees, all of them bearing round green fruits blushed with red. "Once upon a time we had plums, too, but those all died out a while ago."

I moved closer to the trees and touched some of the fruits. They were smooth, and heavy. "The red ones are ready to eat?"

"The red ones, yes." Brian stepped closer to me, and reached above my head for an apple. "Here," he said, and he presented it to me. "This one's perfect."

I put my hand on top of his. "I have never met anyone like you, Brian Murphy."

"Is that a good—" Something behind me caught Brian's attention. "Do you have any people up here? Because that bloke skulking about near my porch is dressed close to how you were on the beach."

I spun around, and saw a man wearing the armour of Kilstiffen's guard creeping around the back of Brian's house with his dagger drawn. Gods below, one of Seamus's men had followed me above.

"They followed me," I whispered, and I drew Brian deeper into the orchard. "I need a weapon."

"He hasn't seen us." Brian stood behind me with his arm around my shoulders and his chest pressed against my back, and he spoke close to my ear. "We can wait him out."

"You don't understand." I turned to face him. "If he followed me here, it was by magic, and he'll keep searching for me that way. If he finds the slightest trace of me, he'll keep coming back. I can't let your home be compromised, and I won't let him find me."

Brian stroked his hand over my hair, his palm coming to rest on the back of my neck. It was an oddly intimate gesture, especially since we'd only known each other for a day. "What do you need from me?"

"Just stay behind me. And are you rather attached to these wine glasses?"

He looked down at our glasses. "Not really."

"Good."

I handed him my glass, then I tied a knot in my skirt in order to shorten the hem to above my knees. That seen to, I took the glass back from him and moved toward the interloper. The man hadn't seen me yet, which was good.

I stubbed my toe on a rock. Swallowing my curses, I picked up the rock as I crept closer to the man. When I was about ten paces from the enemy, I lobbed it straight at his head.

I screamed as I threw it, the motion sending fiery pain through my injured shoulder. Despite the pain, my aim was true, and the rock struck the side of his head. He landed face first on the gravel path. I pulled him onto his back as I smashed the bowl off the glass, ready to slit his throat and silence him permanently.

I paused, my hand wavering above his throat, and realized he was unconscious. I'd thrown the rock with more force than I'd realized. This was a better outcome, since now I wouldn't have to kill him. Regardless of who'd sent him after me, killing a countryman made my belly sour.

"Aoife," Brian called, as he ran toward me. "Are you all right?"

"I am," I replied. "He's out. Still alive," I added.

"What do we do with him now?" Brian asked.

"I can sing away his recent memory," I said, as I got to my feet. "But we will need to remove him from here before he wakes, or it will all be for nothing. If you have some rope, I can fashion a sled, and drag him someplace."

"You don't need to drag him." Brian's face was bloodless as he stared at the unconscious warrior. "We can put him in the back of the car."

"Car?"

"It's like a horse and cart without the horse. Wait here."

I'd seen those mortal conveyances many times, but hadn't known what they were called. Brian walked off, and I realized that whatever had been happening between us while we stood underneath the apple trees was over. He now saw me for what I truly was: a cold-blooded warrior who would kill to defend her home, and her family.

Brian brought his car around, and I watched as he loaded the unconscious man into the back. Normally I would have helped, but my shoulder rendered me all but useless for lifting things. That done, I took a seat in the car beside Brian, and he started down the road.

"You said you can sing his memory away?" Brian asked. It was the first time he'd spoken since he said he would get the car.

"I can only affect his recent memories," I replied. "If my throat wasn't as strained as it is, I could influence him to go all the way home, but removing his memory of your home should do."

"Could you make me do things, with that voice of yours?"

"I could," I replied softly. I'd heard the question he'd left unsaid. Brian worried I'd compelled him to do things, and the prospect of losing his trust unsettled me more than the encounter with Seamus's man. "However, the magic only lasts while we're singing, which is why I'm limited to erasing what's happened to him in the last few hours or so. To do anything more would require several merrows acting in concert."

"Will you remove my memories of you?"

"No. Unless..." I thought of the past day, and how my appearance in Brian's life had turned his world upside down. He would be much safer if he forgot about me... And I wanted him to be safe. "Is that what you'd like me to do?"

"No." Brian took my hand, and his gentle touch reassured me as much as his words. "I'd like to keep my memories of you. All of them."

Images of Home

At Aoife's suggestion, I drove toward a stretch of shoreline that was usually deserted. She claimed her powers were strongest near the sea, and what with her strained voice, she needed all the help she could get. I wondered when I'd started believing her.

It wasn't that I hadn't believed her at any point, more that I was reserving judgement until more facts had presented themselves. Now, in addition to the woman I found on a beach no one could swim to, I had an unconscious man dressed like a medieval warrior in the back of my car. Soon, Aoife would use her magic voice and make his memories of her and my home evaporate like so much morning dew. The unconscious man was a fact, and Aoife's amazing voice was also a fact. These facts were piling up, and I wasn't sure I wanted to deal with any of them.

I stole a look at Aoife. She was as still as a statue, with her hands clenched in her lap so tightly her knuckles were white. As much as she was a fighter—she'd proved that when she took down the man now snoring in my back seat—she was also concerned. For her people, for whatever this plot was she'd stumbled into, and for me. Aoife had almost killed a man to keep me safe.

Since I had hold of the steering wheel in my own white knuckled grip, I stretched my fingers and tried to sift through my thoughts. Aoife was a warrior, that much was true. She was from somewhere far off, but was she a princess? Was she really from a kingdom under the sea?

"Tell me about your home," I said, desperate to learn the truth of her. "Why did it sink?"

"We never sank, not like a ship. We went below of our own volition," she replied. "Times past, the mortals won Ireland above, and the gods claimed Ireland below. At first, that was all well and good, but people kept ending up where they didn't belong. With Kilstiffen being below the mortal lands, but above the gods' home, we're a portal between the two. We keep them safe from each other."

"Then those below Kilstiffen are trapped?"

"Not exactly. There are ways to move between the two lands; we merrows know the ways. Kilstiffen also rises once every seven years, though that may change soon." When she paused, I glanced at her, saw her staring out the window toward the sea. "There's a man in our army who wants to permanently raise Kilstiffen. He thinks that by doing that, he will be able to control both those above and below."

"But you disagree with him."

"I do," she said softly. "I took an oath to defend the city, and those who reside beneath it. If Kilstiffen stays atop the sea permanently, untold harm will come to everyone involved. I can't let that happen."

Her integrity, and devotion to her people awed me. I wanted to pledge myself to Aoife then and there, swearing to stand by her and help her deal with this threat and anything else that befell her people. But that was a fool's idea, wasn't it? Aoife was strong and capable. She didn't need a half-assed fisherman hanging around. And yet, now that I'd spent some time with Aoife, I couldn't imagine living without her.

But first, I needed to get this unconscious man out of my car and out of our lives.

"We're here." I pulled off the road and parked, then we dragged the warrior out of the back of the car and laid him out on the sand. Luckily, there was no one taking a walk along the shore, because we would have had an awful time explaining this. "Is this one a merrow, like you?"

"I'm not sure," she said. "Not all in Kilstiffen are merrows. Either way, he'll wake with no memory of you, or your home."

Aoife knelt next to the man, laid her hand across his eyes, and began to sing. It was a wordless melody that nevertheless created images of an island kingdom in my mind's eye.

"How... How is this happening?" I asked, breathless from the images racing by. "Where are these images coming from?"

"My song is showing you Kilstiffen," she replied, then she resumed her singing, and I resumed watching the pictures of her island home. It was an island filled with castles crowned with tall golden spires, and crushed abalone shell walkways, and surrounded by the deep, dark sea. As she sang, I saw Kilstiffen as clearly as if I was there myself, then I saw the man's memories of my house flit by the backs of my eyelids.

I realised what Aoife was doing. As she pulled out the warrior's memories of my place, she replaced them with his recollections of his own home.

"Brilliant," I whispered.

When her song ended, Aoife took a deep breath and got to her feet. "That ought to take care of it," she began, but the magic of her voice still swirled inside my mind and prickled along my skin. Unable to stop myself, I grabbed her shoulders and kissed her. Her lips were soft, and sweet, and damn it all, I felt like I'd been waiting for this kiss my entire life. Even so, my mind was taken over by one clear thought:

God Almighty, I hope she won't stab me for this.

ROASTED POTATOES AND A SUNSET

I have no idea why this man kissed me.

As soon as I was upright, Brian grabbed my shoulders and hauled me against him. I'd half expected him to mash his mouth against mine like some brute, but he was gentle. Tender even. I'd thought he might taste like apples, or the wine we'd had in the orchard, but he didn't. He was strong, and confident, and so amazingly him, that my senses could barely comprehend what was happening.

Brian was kissing me, and I never wanted him to stop.

Mind you, he was clutching my arms so hard my right shoulder was screaming in pain, and we needed to get away from the unconscious warrior before he came to his senses and saw us, thus undoing all the work I'd done singing away his memories.

I didn't mention any of those things. I slid my arms around his neck, and kissed him back.

Despite my silence, he realized how hard he was holding me. "I'm sorry, I'm hurting you," he said, as he relaxed his grip.

"It's all right." I set my hand on his chest, right over his heart. "You didn't hurt me."

He caressed my hair. "You're certain? And you're not going to stab me for that?"

I rose up on my toes and pecked his lips. "I'm certain, and I won't stab you." I felt his lips stretch into a smile. "But we should move on before he wakes."

"All right, then." Brian took my hand from his chest, and kissed my fingertips. "Let's get back to our dinner. Hopefully, we haven't been gone so long it's reduced down to cinders."

I'd forgotten all about the food waiting for us. We got into the car, and Brian reached into the back and grabbed a hooded garment. "What's this?" I asked, when he deposited it on my lap.

"You're cold," he said.

"I'm fine," I began, but he shook his head.

"Your arms are all gooseflesh," he said. "You can wear that, if you like."

Now that he mentioned it, I was cold, and I slid my arms into the jacket. It was a dark brown, and the interior of the garment was wonderfully soft and warm. Everything Brian owned was warm and soft, which was so unlike what I was used to. I only ever wore my hard armour, the metal and mail cold to the touch, or my stiff leather boots. Even the stone walls and floors of my bedchamber were perpetually chilled. "This is better. Thank you."

"You're quite welcome," he said, as he navigated the village roads. "Aoife, your voice is amazing."

I smiled, flush with pride. "I have one of the strongest voices in all Kilstiffen. It's the main reason why—" I shut my mouth. I didn't want to think about Corentin, much less tell Brian about him.

"It helps me as a warrior," I said, instead of mentioning the prince of Ker Ys. "I can fight with my voice and my sword."

"You must be quite formidable in battle."

"I am," I replied, and I wasn't bragging. "I'm one of the youngest to ever attain my rank. Many speculated I got preferential treatment on account of my father, but I earned my titles."

"I've no doubt of that." Brian flashed me a smile, then he turned off the car. "And, we're here."

He was out of the car in an instant, and came around to my side and opened my door for me. I let him take my hand, and he led me down the path and inside his home. Then, he swore.

"What is that smell?" I asked. It was smoky, though I hadn't seen Brian light a fire, and this scent was nothing like wood smoke or peat.

"Our dinner." Brian grabbed a set of gloves and retrieved the pan from the oven. "This is what we get for not shutting the oven off before we dealt with our uninvited guest."

Neither a surprise attack from Kilstiffen or the demise of his precious chicken rattled Brian. He would have made a wonderful warrior. After he set it on the stovetop I peeked over his shoulder, and frowned.

"It's very brown," I said. The chicken was a deep, dark brown, and the sliced vegetables in the bottom of the pan—the dirt clods he'd referred to as potatoes—weren't much better.

"I believe it's salvageable," he said, as he prodded the bird.

"I don't know about that," I said, then to my utter horror my belly grumbled so loudly Brian heard it.

"I suppose that's our answer," Brian said, and he grabbed a few plates. "Would you please open another bottle of wine for us in your special way?"

I couldn't tell if he was teasing me or not, and in that moment I didn't care. My hunger had overridden everything else, so I selected a bottle from the wine rack and retrieved my sword.

"What happened to the last bottle?" I asked, as I lined up my strike. "We only had two glasses."

"I put the open bottle in the fridge, but this meat looks rather dry," he said as he scooped portions of food onto our plates. "This will definitely be a two bottle meal."

I whacked off the top of the bottle. "Such indulgence," I murmured, as I sheathed my sword. "At home if I have more than a sip of wine everyone treats me like a drunkard."

"Here you can drink the whole bottle, if you like," Brian said. He'd moved on from our plates and was stirring together a sauce. "Although you'll wake up with a mighty headache."

I smiled at his humour, then I picked up the bottle top and handed it to him. He gave it a funny look, then he set it aside and pulled out my chair. "The food's ready, if you are."

I sat, starved and eager to try our meal regardless of how overcooked Brian claimed it was. As for him he was in no rush, and paused to caress my shoulder. "How's it feeling, especially after you lobbed that rock at the man's head?" he asked.

"It's sore," I replied. "Not as much as it was back on the beach, though. As soon as my voice is healed up a bit more, I'll sing the rest of the pain away. I wasted whatever progress I'd made removing that other one's memories," I added.

"You can heal yourself?" He retrieved two earthenware mugs with handles and poured the wine. I imagined he was out of glasses, after earlier. "I suppose you've no need of doctors, then."

"We have healers," I replied. "They're amazing, and can bring a warrior back from the brink of death. But I was trained to tend my own injuries, mostly so I wouldn't be incapacitated around an enemy." Brian asked me something about my training, but the scent of the food had me thoroughly distracted from anything he was going on about. I tried the chicken, which was about how I'd expected roasted meat to taste. The potatoes, however, those were a thing of beauty.

"We have no foods like this below," I said around mouthfuls of potatoes. Leaving all propriety behind, I ate them as fast as I could. "This is the best food I've ever eaten."

"Is it, now." Brian served me the rest of the potatoes from the roasting pan, and then he gave me the few from his plate, and I consumed every morsel.

"I don't know how I will ever repay you," I said, after the last of the potatoes were in my belly. "You got me off that beach, gave me a place to rest, and now you've fed me the most wonderful food. Thank you, Brian. Truly."

He smiled and ducked his head. As wonderful and competent as he was, he was also modest. "Would you like to sit in the garden? We can leave the washing up for later."

"That sounds lovely."

Brian grabbed the bottle of wine while I carried the mugs to a small table and a few chairs set on a wooden platform next to the garden, and there we sat.

"It's so peaceful here," I said, as I burrowed into the warm coat Brian had given me in his car. "Everything is slower, and warmer. Even this garment lends a bit of ease."

"Is life tough down in Kilstiffen?"

"It isn't a particularly hard life, but we're not as generous with our comforts. The amount of sunlight alone up here feels decadent."

"It's sunlight you crave? Well, then, come with me." Brian stood and extended his hand, and I clasped it yet again and let him lead me deeper into his garden. I'd never let a man lead me anywhere in my entire life, but every time Brian took a step, I followed him. This time, we climbed a small hill and turned toward the west, and I gasped.

The sun was setting over the ocean, and the sky was alight in oranges and reds.

"I come to this spot from time to time to watch the sunset," Brian said.

"It's the most beautiful thing I've ever seen."

"I'm seeing something far more beautiful right now."

I turned to Brian, and saw him watching me. "You cannot possibly mean me," I said, as my face warmed. Not only was I allowing this man to lead me around, he'd made me blush.

"Aoife, you are a vision," he said, as he stroked my hair back from my face. "I cannot imagine a more perfect sight than you."

I didn't speak, and instead slid my arms around Brian's waist. He gathered me against his chest, and we stood together as the sun set over the sea. While I took in the spectacle, I considered how one day on the surface had made me happier than I'd ever been in Kilstiffen. What's more, all of my happiness was due to Brian. From the moment he'd set foot on that beach something inside me had changed. It was as if the gate to my heart had unlatched and invited him inside.

I tightened my arms around Brian, and he kissed the top of my head. I had no idea what would become of the two of us, but I was certain of one thing. While Kilstiffen would always be my home, I wanted to stay on the surface, at least for a little while. Then, I would have to return below and deal with everything I'd left undone.

HOOK, LINE, AND SINKER

Early the next morning, I entered my bedroom to wake Aoife. I'd just heard some unwelcome but not wholly unexpected news, and I needed to share it with her as soon as possible. When I found her lying in bed, I forgot everything except how incredibly stunning she was.

After we'd watched the sunset I'd given Aoife full use of my bedroom, and slept across the hall in Donna's old place. The mattress in my sister's room was stiff and lumpy, and the room's air was dusty and stale with disuse. I could have slept in any of the other, better aired guest rooms, or on the couch in the front room instead. For that matter I could have slept in my own bed, but it was plain that Aoife was exhausted. That, coupled with her injuries, meant she needed my room more than I did. As for why I stayed in Donna's room, well, it was the closest to where Aoife lay.

I found her sleeping on her stomach, with her buttercup pale hair spread around her like a halo. I'd been serious when I told her I couldn't imagine a more perfect sight than her face lit up by the setting sun, yet here she was in my bed and my heart almost couldn't take it. Every time I looked at her, she was somehow more beautiful than she had been a moment before.

"Aoife." I gently touched her uninjured shoulder. "Aoife, love. I need to talk to you."

She turned her head toward me, and slowly blinked her eyes open. "Hello," she said. "I've a bone to pick with you."

"Is that so?" I asked, unable to keep from smiling. "Please, tell me how I have offended you."

"You kept something from me." I was a moment from proclaiming my innocence, then she sat up and my mouth forgot how to speak. Aoife was wearing a very tight, very thin sleeveless white shirt, and it was a chore to refrain from staring at her body. "I have discovered that this is your room, and therefore this is your bed."

"Both of those facts are true, and I wasn't keeping either of them from you," I said.

"Where did you sleep?"

"Across the hall," I replied. "I wanted to stay close, in case you needed me."

"You're very kind." Her hand snaked across the bed and rested on mine. "You said you need to talk to me?"

I grasped her fingers. "Before I collected you from the beach, I called your location in to the Coast Guard. When they went by you weren't there, and now I'm being accused of making a false report."

"Bureaucracy up here is as bad as it is in Kilstiffen," Aoife muttered. "How do we fix this?"

"It was strongly suggested that I bring you down to the garda station so you can give your side of the story," I replied. "However, that begs the question of what you will actually tell them."

"I'll tell them the truth," Aoife said. "I will tell them I was stranded, and that you rescued me, and…" She frowned. "I suppose they'll want to know where I came from."

"That they will." My gazed dipped to her throat. "Could you sing a bit, perhaps make them believe you're not a warrior from down below? We should give them a fake name, as well."

"Does my name sound so foreign?"

"What if someone from below came by looking for an Aoife?" I countered. "You said you would remain above until you saw fit to return."

"You're right, I did say that. All right, Brian, what would you like to call me?"

I thought about her magical voice, and suggested, "Why not Calliope?"

"The Greek muse," she murmured, as her cheeks darkened. "It means beautiful voice."

"Aye." I kissed her knuckles. "That it does, and it suits you rather well."

Aoife turned away, but not before I saw her blush creep all the way down her neck. "All right, then. I'll be Calliope for these guards of the coast. When should we leave?"

"Honestly, the sooner we get this over with, the better."

After Aoife got ready for the day, we went straight down to the garda and put her new name to use. I told the story exactly as it had happened to me, that I spotted a woman stranded on a beach below the cliffs and rescued her. As for Aoife, she claimed to be one Calliope Kearney, and that she had been on holiday with her family when she became separated from them and ended up on the beach. It was a flimsy story, but the guards were just as captivated by Aoife as I was. They fell for the tale hook, line, and sinker, even though she sang nary a note.

"That wasn't nearly as awful as you made it out to be," Aoife said, after we left the station. She was wearing another one of Donna's old dresses, though this one was pink with tiny flowers scattered across it. On top of the dress, she had on my brown sweatshirt I'd given her the night before, and I had to admit that I liked it when she wore my clothes.

"Believe me, I was prepared for the worst." Instead of me being formally charged with filing a false report and possibly fined, I was lauded as a hero for rescuing her. "I didn't dare hope the guards would fall victim to your charms, as I most certainly have."

She glanced at me over her shoulder and smiled, then she turned her face toward the sky. "We have another sunny day. Do the clouds ever come in?"

"We get rain more often than not," I said. "This has just been a stretch of good weather." We turned the corner, and I spied the pub. "Let's stop in for a pint and a bite."

"A bite of what? Do they have any potatoes?"

"I'm sure we can find something with potatoes for you."

When we entered the pub, I saw the house band setting up, and I realized it was Thursday; they always supplied music for the lunch crowd on that day. Ever since I'd first spied Aoife's golden form on the beach I'd lost all sense of time and space, save for how it related to her. I moved to take a seat at the bar, but Aoife placed her hand on my arm.

"Can we sit near the stage?" she asked. "I'm interested to hear what sort of songs these musicians create."

"We surely can." I swiped two lunch menus from the bar, and let Aoife select a table for us. Once we were seated, I slid a menu toward her, and paused. "Do you know how to read English? I can read it to you, if you like."

"Of course, I can read English, along with several other languages," she said, and she snatched the menu away from me. "We believe in knowing as much as we can about the surface so we can blend in whenever we need to come above."

"Yes, you didn't stand out at all in your gold chain mail."

Aoife sniffed. "That was an unexpected journey, of which you're well aware."

After we perused the menu, and Aoife told me that she was willing to try anything that came with potatoes and didn't contain fish, I went up to the bar to order. A friend of mine, Lucas Sullivan, was seated at the prime corner spot.

"You've deigned to join us at the pub?" I said, by way of greeting. Lucas was a professional athlete and owned the local surf shop. He also avoided alcohol, claimed it was on account of his training. "Has hell frozen over?"

"Bridgette's craving fish and chips," he replied. Bridgette was his wife, and she was carrying their second child. "This place has the best, so here I am. Who's the blonde?" he asked, jerking his chin toward Aoife.

"I found her stranded on a beach, and now she's staying with me."

"You're kidding," Lucas said. "You living in a fairy tale out on that boat?"

"So it seems," I replied, then the bartender came by and took my order.

"Looks like your beach girl's getting ready to sing," Lucas said.

I turned, and saw Aoife speaking with the musicians. They were handing her what looked to be lyric sheets. "Yes, looks like she is."

"Her voice any good?"

"Lucas, you have no idea."

Half an hour later, and Aoife had every person in the pub eating out of the palm of her hand.

She'd only regaled us with a few songs, but a few was all it took. Beginning with the very first note she sang we all stared at her in rapt attention, only moving in order to applaud and demand more songs. As for me, I couldn't tell you what words she sang or what these songs were about, other than they were beautiful. I did, however, wonder why her voice was strong enough to enchant a room full of strangers, but she couldn't heal a wee bruise atop her shoulder.

After her third song, our food was delivered to our table. Seeing that our lunch was ready Aoife handed off the microphone and joined me at our table. "That was exhilarating," she said.

"You've gotten yourself a following," I said, as I nodded toward the rest of the room. Aoife peeked over her shoulder, and ducked her head when several patrons waved at her.

"My people say music was the world's first language," she said, then she focused on our meals. "What have you gotten us?"

"This is called a shepherd's pie," I said, as I slid the hot casserole dish toward her. "As you can see, it features potatoes."

"Excellent," she said, then she spied my plate. "That doesn't look like chicken."

"That's because it's lamb stew," I replied. "Would you like to try some?"

"Perhaps later," she said, then she tucked into her shepherd's pie. Our meals were excellent, but then the pub's food was always top notch.

After we'd finished our lunches, we spent the afternoon talking over our pints. Aoife told me about her family, beginning with her sister Scáthach, who was a warrior and a teacher, and her brother Oscar, who was somewhat of a clown. Aoife's father, the king of Kilstiffen, was called Steinar the Immoveable, though she claimed he was a kind and just man. I didn't see how a just man was also immoveable, but I kept that observation to myself.

"And what of your hopes and dreams, Brian Murphy?" she asked. "Once you have your farm up and running, and your restaurant serving the best plates on the island, then what?"

"Then? Oh, you're assuming I can get that first bit done."

"Of course you can." She slid her hand across the table and grasped mine. "You're a fighter just as much as I am, but your weapon of choice is a cooking pot. Still good to bash someone's head in," she added, and we laughed. "But I'm sure you'll put yours to better use than that."

"Perhaps." I rubbed my thumb across her knuckles. Her hands were small and fine boned, yet they wielded a wickedly sharp sword. Or, as they'd done the day prior, a rock and a broken wineglass. "As for what I'd like after the farm and restaurant, I'd like a family. I want a partner, so I'm not alone all the time, and children, so I've someone to teach and spoil the way my parents taught and spoiled me."

"You want a life," Aoife said. "I would like one of those, but I was born to defend Kilstiffen."

I leaned close to her, and asked, "Who says you can't have both?"

Aoife set her palm against my face, with her thumb gently stroking my cheek. Then she saw something across the room and froze. "Foolishness," she hissed.

I blinked. "What's foolish?"

"I am the fool, for singing as I did," she replied, then she jerked her chin toward the door. "Brian. Those men."

I twisted around in my chair and had a look at these men that so affected Aoife. There were three of them standing just inside the entrance, each of them wearing nondescript and utterly plain brown clothing. They were trying so hard to blend in, they ended up standing out like sore thumbs. "What of them?"

"They're from my father's guard," she said. "I fear they've come above looking for me. They must have heard me, and followed my voice into the pub."

"And what if they were sent by your father? You left in a flurry and haven't returned. He's probably worried about you."

Aoife bit her lip. "Perhaps. Is there another way out?"

I pointed toward the back of the room. "We can leave through the kitchen. Wait for me near the swinging doors while I settle the bill."

She nodded, and went toward the kitchen while I went to the bar and paid for our lunches. That done, I took her hand and we slipped through the kitchen and out to the alley behind the pub.

"Why are you hiding from your father?" I asked.

"I'm not hiding," she bit off. "But I don't want to go back. Not yet, not while that villain Seamus has his ear, and he's actually considering leaving the portal open permanently."

"Exactly what would happen if the portal was open?" When she didn't answer, I continued, "You said the gods reside below Kilstiffen. Surely they won't harry us mortals too much."

"But mortals will also be able to harry them," Aoife said. "They're not all gods down below. Some are just people."

Her concern about those below Kilstiffen made me realise something. "Who are you protecting?"

"My mother, and my brother," she replied. "Oscar was a bit of a handful, so my father sent him below some time ago."

"And why is your mother there?" I asked. "Did she pass on to the land of the dead?"

"No. She belongs there." We reached the mouth of the alley, and Aoife halted. "Brian, they're up ahead!"

The three men from below were making their way down the street toward us, and they appeared to be asking questions of anyone willing to talk to them. Part of me wondered if I should flag them down, and get whatever was happening between Aoife and her father out in the open and settled. Then the leader of the three turned, and I saw a sword strapped across his back. A quick glance told me the other two were similarly armed, and Aoife had left her sword at home. She was a strong fighter, but I didn't like the odds of her going up against three armed men.

If she was overpowered and they captured her, they would take her below, and I might never see her again. I couldn't let that happen.

"We must flee," she whispered.

"If we run we'll attract their attention." I faced her, and cupped her cheek with my hand. "What we need is for them to overlook us. Do you trust me?"

She put her hand on top of mine. "I do, Brian. I trust you with my life."

I watched her for a moment, but I saw no fear or apprehension in her eyes. Hoping I wasn't about to shatter the fragile trust we'd built together, I drew her close and kissed her. Objectively, my reasoning was sound. Those men were looking for a warrior and a king's daughter, not a woman snogging in an alley behind a pub. In truth, I'd been dying to kiss her again.

Aoife was startled, and yelped softly as my mouth covered hers. But she didn't push me away, and nor did she put up any other defenses. Instead, she kissed me back with such fervor I slid my hands down her back and to her thighs, then I lifted her against the wall, so we were more of a height. With my hips braced against hers, I kissed her as if my life depended on it.

When we parted I rested my forehead against hers. My heart was racing, as were my thoughts, and I had no idea what would happen next. What I did know was that if those men from below tried to take Aoife against her will, they would have to go through me.

"That was your grand idea?" she asked, as she twined her arms around my neck.

"I had a few ideas, but I liked that one best." I cupped her cheek, and stroked her smooth, soft skin. I was certain I would never get enough of her. "Was it a good plan?"

"It seems to have worked." Aoife peeked around my shoulder. "They've gone."

I nodded, but made no move to release her. "You're sure?"

"I'm sure." She moved so her feet were on the ground, then she leaned up and kissed me. "Take me home? We... we should talk."

"Aye. Let's go home."

HEARTS CALL OUT

B rian was quiet as we walked back to his home, and I couldn't fault him for it. He'd picked up me up as a stranded woman on a beach, and now there were armed men skulking about the village searching for me. If he had a drop of sense, he would turn me out, and not be bothered with me or my problems ever again.

Gods below, I hope that isn't what comes to pass.

When we entered the house, I began, "I'm sure you have many questions."

"Why is your voice strong enough to remove a man's memories, and enchant an entire pub, yet you still haven't healed your shoulder?" he asked. "Surely one such as you could handle a wee bruise."

I glanced at him and then away, then I sang a single clear note. "I didn't want to heal my shoulder," I admitted, then I tugged the neck of my dress to the side and revealed my unmarked skin. "You're right, I could have healed it earlier."

"Why didn't you? Surely it was painful."

"I didn't want to go back," I said. "If I was still hurt, I had a reason to remain above."

Brian nodded. "Are you a criminal?"

"No!" I approached him, and placed my hands on his chest. He kept his hands to himself. "No. I've broken no laws, neither here nor below."

"Then why were those men searching for you?" he pressed.

"I told you, there was a fight and I left." I resolved to tell him everything, and continued, "There were two fights, actually. During the first, my father betrothed me to a prince."

Brian went still. "You're to be married?"

"No." I stepped back from Brian, and shook my head. "I don't want to be betrothed."

"If you don't want to be, how did it come to pass?"

"It all happened so fast." I took a breath, and remembered how normal everything had seemed that day, and how quickly everything had changed. "I woke up the morning of my eighteenth birthday, and put on my gear to train as I do every day. My father summoned me, and when I went to him, he was with Gradlon, who is the king of Ker Ys. Also present was Gradlon's younger brother, Corentin."

Brian watched me for a moment, then he gathered me against his chest. Until he had his arms around me, I had no idea how much I needed him to hold me. "Corentin is the prince?" he asked, as he stroked my hair.

"He is."

"What was he like?"

I wanted to tell Brian that Corentin was awful or ugly or stupid, but none of that was the truth. "He is a perfectly nice man, but I don't want to marry him."

"If he's a decent fellow, why not?"

"I don't love him, and if I marry him I'll be trapped with a person I don't love for my entire life." I leaned back so I could meet his eyes. "I don't want a good enough husband. If I decide to marry someone, it will be because I love them so much, I cannot breathe when they're not near me."

"Did you tell your father how you felt?"

"I did. I told him that it wasn't fair, and that I'd never even known Corentin existed before that moment, and how could either of us be expected to go through with a marriage. When I objected, they all treated me as if I was being unreasonable." I squeezed my eyes shut, while images of my father and King Gradlon shouting while Corentin watched me like a starving hawk played behind my eyes. "As if I was something to be bartered away."

Brian tightened his arms around me. "How did you leave it with them?"

"I stormed out of the room, and as I stalked through the palace I found myself in the council chamber. I walked right into Seamus's plot to open the portal permanently, and without the king's knowledge. I accused them of treason, and that's when the second fight broke out."

"And that's how you ended up on the beach," Brian concluded. "You're only eighteen?"

"I am. Is my age a problem?"

"No, no," he said. "Not at all. But I am sorry all of this happened on your birthday."

"My birthday's always been treated like any other day," I said. "But this year, I became marriageable. I stopped being my father's daughter, and became a commodity."

"Here, you're noting of the sort," Brian said. "Up here you're a person, and no one can buy or trade a person." He tucked my hair behind my ear. "This is why you hid from your father's men, instead of talking to them or fighting them off. You thought they'd capture you, and bring you back to the prince."

"I'm sorry I didn't tell you everything right away," I said. "I was afraid that if you knew, you'd be done with me."

"You, afraid? I don't believe it." Brian's hand traveled down my spine to my hip. "You, my beauty, are fearless. Not only that, if those men try to take you, they'll have me to deal with."

"Brian, you can't face off against a company of Kilstiffen's warriors!"

He kissed my hair. "For you, I'll face off against the world."

I rested my cheek against Brian's chest, and wondered why I couldn't be betrothed to a man like him. "I'm so sorry, Brian. I never meant to lay all of my problems at your door."

He tilted up my chin. "Aoife, love, you keep apologizing, but you don't need to. You're here, and that's what matters. We can deal with all of these problems tomorrow."

"We?"

"Aye, we." Brian paused, his face uncertain but tinged with hope. "If you'll have me, that is?"

"H-Have you?"

"We can have a life together," he said. "I realize this is all new for both of us, but ever since I heard your voice floating across the waves, I can think of nothing but you."

I squeezed my eyes shut. "You really heard me?"

"Aye. I heard the most beautiful melody, and it led me right to your beach." He paused, and added, "Although, it couldn't have been you, could it? You injured your voice when you escaped."

"It was me," I whispered. "Among merrows, we have a saying, that our heart calls to our one true mate. You heard me call out to you, even when I wasn't singing."

Brian kissed me, but not like the desperate man he'd been behind the pub. This time, he kissed me as if I was cherished. "Then it truly was love at first sight," he murmured, against my lips.

My breath caught in my throat—and wasn't that what I had just said? I needed a partner I loved so dearly he took my breath away. I would accept nothing less.

I reached up and stroked the back of Brian's neck, then I sunk my fingers into his dark hair. His skin was so warm and smooth, and beneath that glorious skin he was covered in hard muscle. From my own years of training, I understood the amount of activity one needed to build his sort of body, and I imagined him shirtless on his boat hauling fishing nets out of the sea.

No doubt about it. Brian took my breath away, in more ways than one.

"If we do this, it won't be easy," I warned. "Kilstiffen will always be a part of me. I am the guardian of the portal, and I will return to stop Seamus's plot."

He stroked the side of my face. "I accept all of you, Aoife," he said, then he pressed his lips to mine. "I want all of you."

"In that case, Brian Murphy, I'm yours."

Always

I'm yours.

God Almighty, those two little words nearly undid me. Ever since I'd picked Aoife up from that beach, I'd worried that she was only humoring my attraction to her, which would be understandable. She'd needed a place to rest, and I readily offered her my home. Every time she returned one of my smiles, or reached for my hand, I hoped she felt something more than gratitude for me.

Now, I had confirmation.

"All of you?" I asked, because this was the best conversation I'd ever had, and I wanted to prolong it for as long as possible. "Right down to your toes?"

Aoife laughed deep in her throat as she twined her arms around my neck. "You've an interest in my toes?"

"I've an interest in every part of you." I pushed back her hair, and found myself falling into the endless blue of her eyes. "Fitting that you're from the sea. Your eyes are as blue as the ocean on a summer's day."

"Be that as it may, I've my mother's eyes, and she's not a merrow." Aoife bit her lip, and added, "She's from below Kilstiffen. There's so much more I have to tell you about my family."

"Let's start today." I drew her toward the back door. "I can show you the rest of the garden, and while we walk you can tell me all about them."

We stepped outside, and walked toward the orchards on the eastern side. "That's where the plums were," I said, as I pointed toward a few grayish stumps beyond the apple trees.

"Plums," she repeated. "Are those like apples?"

"Not really. On Saturday morning we can go to the market, and pick up a few. We can make a pie."

"Oh, you're going to let me cook again? Am I forgiven for what happened with the chicken?"

"On second thought, perhaps you'd best stick to opening the wine." She laughed, but didn't dispute. Hand in hand, we meandered toward the far side of the garden.

"What's that?" she asked. I followed her gaze, and saw the old wooden fence.

"Once upon a time we kept a few sheep, and that was their pen," I replied. "The barn's long gone."

Aoife wrinkled her nose. "Keeping animals like that must have been a great deal of work."

"Aye, it was, which is why we don't have any now," I said, then I felt a few cold raindrops. "And the sun has decided to nap for a bit."

"Your water comes from the sky," Aoife said, then she turned her face up and spun around in the rain. "Even when the sun isn't in the sky, it's still beautiful."

"As much as you're enjoying this downpour, we'd best get back inside." The last thing either of us needed was to catch a chill. No sooner had we begun walking back than the skies opened up, and we were thoroughly drenched by the time we got inside. Aoife took off my sweatshirt and hung it on the coatrack, then she turned around and I almost had a heart attack.

"What's wrong?" she asked.

"Your dress." It had gotten soaked, and the wet fabric clung to her every curve.

Every. Single. Curve.

"What about my dress?" she asked.

"You should take it off. So you don't get sick," I added. "What have you got on underneath?"

"Nothing. You didn't think I was going to wear another woman's undergarments, did you?"

God Almighty. "There's a robe hanging on the back of the bathroom door," I said, because if I spared another thought about Aoife's wardrobe situation, I might go mad. "You can put that on. It'll keep you nice and warm."

I turned around and walked toward my bedroom. Aoife followed, and walked past me into the bathroom. "This is lovely," she said when she found the robe; it was a heavy plush one, almost as blue as her eyes, and I'd never even worn it. "You don't mind?"

"Not at all." I pulled off my damp jumper, and grabbed a flannel from the closet. "I'm sure it'll look better on you than it ever would on me." As I buttoned my shirt I glanced toward the bathroom, and saw that Aoife had left the door open while she changed. Clearly, this woman wanted my heart to explode. "I'll go make us some tea."

While the tea brewed, I built a fire, and by the time Aoife joined me the front room was warm and cosy. "Such comfort," she said, as she sat on the couch. "You take very good care of me."

"And I always will." I sat beside Aoife and she fit herself against me. Since she was now only wearing the robe, her long, lithe legs were on full display.

"You're so muscular," I said, as I stroked her calf. "When you use your voice to compel others to do things, does it hurt them?"

"I don't think so," she replied. "As far as I know they do things willingly, at least in the moment." She tugged at the edge of my sleeve. "If you're curious, I could compel you to do something small, and harmless. Then you would know."

"All right," I said, because I knew Aoife would never hurt me. The next thing I knew I was standing next to the couch, shirtless and with my belt unfastened.

"What," I began, then Aoife burst out laughing. "Did you compel me to take my clothes off?"

"I did," she said. "You took your shirt off so fast I worried you'd throw it in the fire!"

I picked my shirt up off the floor and tossed it onto a nearby chair, then I reclaimed my spot on the couch. Aoife nestled herself in the crook of my arm, and tilted her head back to ask, "Are you mad at me?"

"Never." I caressed her soft, smooth neck. "I can confirm that your victims feel no pain."

"Not victims. Enemies," she corrected. "Have you been worried about the one whose memories I altered?"

"A bit," I admitted. "Would you have killed him, if necessary?"

"Yes." She twisted around, baring her shoulder in the process. "I will do anything to protect those I love."

I grasped Aoife's hips and moved her around so she faced me. "You love me?"

"Aye. I love you."

I pulled her body up and kissed her between her breasts, all while she squirmed and squealed with laughter. "What was that for?"

"I'm thanking your sweet, perfect heart for calling to me." I settled her against me, then I settled my hand on her arm and stroked her soft skin. "Where can I touch you?"

"Anywhere you'd like," she replied, then she placed her hand on my belt. "I want to see the rest of you."

Since I thought that was more than fair, I set Aoife on the far side of the couch and stood to remove my boots and jeans. She watched me the entire time, her gaze darting from my chest to my legs. When my cock emerged, her eyes widened and she gasped. I remembered her age, and wondered if we should be doing this at all.

"Have you ever seen a man before?" I asked.

She met my gaze. "I have. And I rather like the sight of you." Aoife stood and let the robe fall to the floor, then she set her hands on my chest. "As I said, I'm yours."

I sank a hand into her hair while the other rested on her hip, and I kissed her as if I were drowning and she was my only source of air. "I'm yours, too. Now, and always."

THE MORNING AFTER

I had no idea it could be like this.

I woke up lying in bed with Brian. He was splayed out on his back, his chest rising and falling in a steady rhythm. We'd been up most of the night, talking and kissing and finally making love, and now I was certain that I would never again be so happy.

I stroked his chest, and the ruff of dark hair over his heart. My fingers followed the hair down to his belly to where it disappeared in a dark line below the blanket, and I paused. Did I have the right to touch him in such a way? I didn't want to take ungranted liberties with him. Then I remembered how we'd touched each other last night, and smiled. Those liberties had been granted, many times over.

No matter how I felt about Brian today or any day, eventually I would have to return below. My father wouldn't let up searching for me, and I could hide for only so long. Going home would be best for all concerned, with the exception of the marriage that was waiting for me.

Actually, breaking that betrothal would make me quite happy. So happy that I wanted to start planning the break right away.

I gently shook Brian awake. When he opened his eyes, he smiled at me. "My beauty," he said.

"You remember how I'm betrothed to a prince?"

"And yet, here you are in bed with me," he countered. I laid my cheek against his chest as I slid my arm around his waist.

"I am, and there is no place I would rather be. However, I need to tell my father the marriage to Corentin will not happen."

His fingers danced up my spine. "Will you be safe?"

"Of course," I scoffed, then I recalled how Brian had found me: alone, wounded, and nearly hopeless. "I will tell Father I've found my intended mate, and that will be the end of it."

"You think you'll tell the king of this mighty city that we're meant to be, and he'll find it within his noble heart to never separate a couple in love?" he asked.

"If only it were that easy. He will glower at me, and rage, and I'm sure I'll do my own bit of yelling. However, my parents were a love match, and they fought against people far more powerful than the kings of Kilstiffen and Ker Ys to be together. No, Father won't like what I have to say, but he will understand."

"All right, then. I'll go with you."

"Brian, you can't!"

"I should be standing beside you when you go to your father," he said. "I meant what I said, Aoife. I'll stand between the world and you."

"I know you will," I said softly. "I will bring you below, but not right away. Let things settle a bit, then I will introduce you to my family." I rolled onto my back. "There's also the small matter of treason brewing beneath my father's nose."

"How will we handle that?"

"Truly, I've no idea." I draped my arm across my eyes, and wondered how I would handle any of this.

"You sang to me last night."

I moved my arm and opened my eyes. Brian was up on his elbow, smiling down at me. "I did. My people, we sing when we... um..." Face hot, I rolled toward him and hid against his chest. "I've never sung for anyone before. Not like that."

Brian's arm came around me, and he kissed my shoulder. "Your song was beautiful, just like you."

THE CITY RISES

At first, we decided to wait a few weeks before Aoife returned below; well, she alone made the decision. I just agreed that it was a good one. And wait we did, but at the end of those weeks we decided that she should spend some time training, and rebuilding her strength. That excuse begat another, and another, until nearly four months had passed. In that time Aoife had well and truly become my partner in all things, be they at home, on my boat, or in my heart. As for me, I was happier than I'd ever been.

No one called her Aoife but me, and I only did so when we were alone. Around town she was known as Calliope Kearney, the stranded woman who was rescued by the fisherman. The local folk loved her as I did, and occasionally she joined the band that played at the pub twice a week. She was careful to not join too often, and afterward we laid low for a few days, in case any of her countrymen had heard her song and those below got wind of her location. All was well, for after we evaded the small group of her father's men, no one else came looking for her. It was like we were living in a long, lazy summer of happiness.

Much like the season, all things must come to an end.

"Mo ghrá," Aoife murmured one morning, long before the sun was up. We were still in bed, and I was of a mind to stay there as long as possible. "Can we go to the cliffs today, near where you found me?"

"I don't see why not," I replied. "Why would you like to go there?"

"Kilstiffen's due to rise today, and I want you to see it."

My guts twisted when she told me that, but I kept it to myself. My deepest fear was that her father's guards would find her and snatch her away from me, then Aoife would be married off to that prince and I'd never see her again. I realized that was an irrational fear, since my beauty had fought her way out of there once, and I knew she could do it again. Still, the thought of losing her chilled me.

"Will it be safe?" I asked.

"Of course," she replied. "We'll only watch it from afar, then we can go to the pub for breakfast."

And so it came to pass that we were parked above the sea as the sun rose behind us. Aoife went right up to the cliff's edge, and pointed to a spot on the water. At first, I saw nothing but the choppy sea, then the sun's rays hit the water, and revealed a hint of gold beneath the waves.

"That's it?" I asked.

"It is," she replied, a hint of pride in her voice. Before my eyes an entire city dragged itself up from the depths as if an unseen giant had retrieved it from the bottom of the sea. All of the buildings had gleaming white walls like mother of pearl, and were roofed in gold. Iridescent blue walkways reminiscent of abalone shells twisted among them, and I could see brightly colored gardens and deep green lawns. The city was everything Aoife had described, and more. It was breathtaking.

"Amazing," I muttered. She laughed, and slid her arms around me underneath my coat. Aoife was like a cat, always searching for an extra bit of warmth.

"Did you not believe me?"

"I believed you, but now I see it and that's something different entirely." What was truly amazing was the size of Kilstiffen. It had to be as large as Inisheer, or perhaps even Inis Mór. "People are going to notice this."

"That they shall, but the city won't stay above for long. Soon enough it will descend beneath the waves, and anyone who comes looking won't find a trace of them."

"What if they take pictures?"

Aoife shrugged. "What if they do? It still won't be here."

The next morning Aoife again woke me near sunrise, this time in a near panic. "Brian, it's still there."

"What is?" I mumbled, wondering if she meant the remains of last night's dinner. I had a bad habit of leaving the washing up for the next morning, which drove Aoife crazy.

"Kilstiffen. It didn't descend."

I sat up, and rubbed the sleep from my eyes. "What does that mean?"

"It means something is very, very wrong." Aoife went to the far side of the room and snapped the curtains open. As the sunlight streamed into the room it glinted off her armour, though she had her sword sheathed along her back instead of at her hip. "I need to go back."

"All right." I stood and located my trousers. "What should we bring?"

"I'll go alone. Hear me out," she added, when I opened my mouth. "We don't know what's happening. I will slip in from below the city, learn what I can, and be gone before anyone knows I'm there."

I wanted to argue with her, but I didn't have the right to keep her from her home. What's more, I knew she wouldn't listen to me. I approached her, and slid my hand along the back of her neck. "You're certain you can sneak in and out?"

"I am." She took my hand from her neck, and kissed my knuckles. "I can be there and out and back in bed with you tonight."

I grunted. "That's the first good thing you've said today." I fastened my trousers, then I sat to pull on my boots. "How will you be getting below? The sea?"

"No. I'll descend through the caves."

When Aoife told me she'd be returning to Kilstiffen by way of a cave, I assumed she meant one of the sea caves along the shore. While those would work, she had a much sneakier route in mind, one that began in an inland cave.

"This way, they won't see me coming," she explained. I drove her to the cave in question, all the while questioning if what I was doing was the right thing. Having Aoife in my life was the best thing that had ever happened to me, and while I trusted her implicitly, once she went below I had no way of knowing if she would ever return. And if that Prince Corentin was still hanging around...

"How will your father react to your sudden return?" I asked, instead of bringing up Corentin. "I imagine he'll be a bit sore after all this time."

"That he will be," she murmured. "But he said himself I'm no longer a child, which means I can come and go as I please. At least, that's how I interpret it."

"I'm sure he'll be glad to know you're safe." We had reached the cave entrance, so I pulled off the road and parked. Aoife shot me a glance when I moved to exit the car. "I'll walk you to the entrance, if that's all right."

"Of course, it is." She held out her hand and I grasped it, then we followed the well-worn path right down to the crack in the earth.

"You're sure this is the way?"

"I am." Aoife turned into me, and I gathered her against my chest. "I'm coming back, Brian. I'll always come back to you."

"When you return, marry me."

"Aye." She leaned back, her face taken over by the loveliest smile. "When I return, I will marry you, Brian Murphy."

EATING, IS IT?

The first thing I accomplished on my return below was to fall on my arse in the dark, slippery cave. Why I hadn't thought to grab the torch Brian kept in the car was beyond me. At least no one was around to witness me splayed out in the mud. I got myself up, and followed the old tunnel to the edge of the city. This network of tunnels was a remnant of an older land, and wasn't used by much of anyone nowadays. When I was a wee thing my siblings and I had often played in the tunnels, hiding from each other and our minders in turn. As a result, I knew every nook and cranny in this stone warren, save for that new patch of mud I'd slipped on.

I rested my hand against the cave wall, and paused for a breath. Brian wanted to marry me. What's more, I wanted to marry him. All I had to do was determine why the city remained aloft, fix things in either a magical or mundane manner, and then I could return to Brian and we would never be parted again. Which meant I needed to get moving.

Soon enough I was in the city proper, and I found every last resident celebrating. They were out in the streets cheering and waving colored flags, and singing so loudly the entire surface world could hear them. We usually celebrated the return of the sun, but not in such a raucous manner. I couldn't remember any holidays occurring around this time of year, and I had no idea what they were going on about. I flagged down a soldier, and asked him what was happening.

"We're not doomed to exist at the bottom of the sea any longer," he replied. "We'll stay on the surface from now on, as our own island! Isn't it wonderful news?"

"Aye," I murmured, while my heart fell. Seamus had found a way to keep the city aloft, and my father had obviously gone along with his mad plan. I thanked the soldier and sent him on his way, then I did exactly what I didn't want to do. I went to the royal palace.

Getting inside was simple enough—as Steinar's daughter no guard could refuse me entry—and went straight to my rooms. All those that had seen me merely nodded a greeting, which was fitting. Hopefully I would be gone before any of them mentioned having set eyes on me to my father. All was going to plan until I was inside my chamber, and my attendant, Talia, ran out of my wardrobe and nearly scared the life out of me.

"Aoife," she squealed when she saw me. "Where have you been? I've been worried sick about you!"

"I'm fine," I began, and Talia threw herself into my arms. She'd been charged with my care shortly after I was born, and when my mother returned below, she effectively filled that role for me. "I'm sorry. I never meant to make you worry."

"I know you'd never do that." She drew back, and held my face in her hands, just like she'd done when I was a child. "Are you here for the feast?"

"There's to be a feast? For what?"

"The king ordered it," she said. "We're to live as an island from now on."

"So I heard." Talia began bustling about the chamber, selecting a gown and shoes for me to wear to the celebration. I was about to tell her to stop, when I realized that appearing as the dutiful daughter at my father's side may be the perfect way for me to figure out what Seamus had done, and how to undo it. "Who else will be attending this celebration?"

"The entire city will be there," Talia began, then she faced me. "You left because of what happened with Corentin, didn't you?"

"No." I glanced at her. "Not entirely."

"He's still here," she said. "Gradlon returned to Ker Ys some time ago, but Corentin declared he would wait for his bride's return," she added, with a knowing glance at me.

"Gods below," I grumbled. "As if we have some sort of great love between us. I've only ever seen him once. I might not even recognize him if I saw him again."

"You will. He's the annoying one who won't leave Steinar's side." Talia had always spoken freely when it was just the two of us. It was one of the things I appreciated most about her. She selected a deep green gown from the depths of my wardrobe and held it out with a flourish. "Let's dress you up like the goddess you are, and give him a taste of what he's missing."

I couldn't help it, I laughed. "Yes, lets."

"Are you sure this is my dress?" I asked, as Talia laced up the back. "None of my clothes are this tight."

"The dress is the same size, but you've gotten bigger," she replied, as she gave the laces another yank. "Especially in your belly."

"I have been eating well," I said, as I recalled the many decadent meals Brian had prepared for me; cakes and pies and his amazing roasted potatoes. Those meals were why I hadn't been able to wear my sword belt about my hips, and had fashioned it into a sheath on my back.

"Eating, is it." Talia came around to the front of me, and took my hands. "Come here, to the mirror. Now stand sideways." She pulled the fabric tight around my midsection, and revealed a small bump.

"Och, I hadn't realized I'd indulged so much," I began, the Talia placed her hand on my belly and sang.

"Aoife. This belly isn't from eating too many cakes." My skin warmed underneath her hand, and I recalled that before Talia had been tasked with rearing the royal children, she was a midwife. "Feel that?"

"Aye," I said, staring at her hand. "What does it mean?"

"It seems you're with child."

"W-What?" I reached toward my reflection, then I looked down at my belly. Brian had loved me well, and often, and here was the proof of it. "Oh. Oh, that makes sense. Are you certain?"

"I've never been wrong." Talia took my hands. "Tell me, where have you been all this time? Are you certain you're all right?"

"Yes," I said, as tears streamed down my cheeks. "I'm so happy, and once I tell Brian about the baby he will be happy as well."

"Brian?"

"Yes, Brian is who I've been with above. I've spent every day with him ever since I left." I watched my reflection as I set my hand on the small curve near my waist. "When I return to him, we're to be married."

Talia snorted. "If he's not Corentin, I like him already. Does Steinar know about this impending marriage?"

"Not yet, and won't this add some excitement to the feast."

GOING BELOW

After Aoife disappeared into the cave, I sat in the car staring at the dark opening for what felt like half of forever. My time would have been better served returning home, or going down to the harbour to perform some maintenance on my boat. Staring at a cave entrance was a foolish waste of time, and I knew it. But Aoife—fearless, fearless Aoife—had gone into that cave, and I couldn't look away until she came back out.

What if she never returns?

I shut my eyes and laid my forehead against the steering wheel. Aoife had promised she would come back to me, and I believed her. With my whole heart I believed her, but her return wasn't only up to my beauty. I knew Kilstiffen had an army, and a bloke called Seamus who was Aoife's enemy, and a king who was Aoife's father. The king alone could keep her from coming back to me, never mind all the other obstacles she would have to face.

I couldn't let her do it alone.

I reached under the passenger seat and grabbed the torch I kept for emergencies, then I opened the glove box and rooted around until I found my utility knife. Light and weaponry sorted, I plunged into the cave and set after Aoife.

The cave was about what I expected it to be, dark and musty smelling. Thanks to the torch it was easy enough to find my way, and it wasn't too long before I thought I'd jumped the gun coming down here. Of course, Aoife could navigate her way through this cave and down to Kilstiffen. She'd probably walked this path a hundred times before, and could do it in her sleep. I'd almost convinced myself to return to the car, when the torch's beam caught something shining on the cave floor. I crouched down to investigate, and felt fear wrap its cold fingers around my heart.

Lying on the mud on the cave floor was a triangle of gold chain mail. Aoife's mail.

Had she been in a fight, and been injured? What sort of blow must her adversary have landed to break off a piece of her mail? I remembered her telling me that while it was plated in pure gold, the rings themselves were iron.

I stuffed the mail into my pocket, angled the torch's beam ahead of me, and set off down the tunnel. My Aoife needed me, and by God I would find her.

I followed the cave to a large open gallery, on the far side of which was an old wooden gate. Thanks to my knife I got the door opened, then I stepped through the entrance and found myself in Kilstiffen proper.

And realised that I was in far, far over my head.

Being that the city was still atop the waves, it was filled with glorious sunlight. All that light revealed the houses, bridges, and dozens or maybe even hundreds of residents going about their business. Each one of them was dressed like a lord or lady, with clothing of silk and velvet. Not a one wore an old jumper and jeans, like me.

"Is there no working class here?" I muttered. I kept to the shadows as best I could, all the while wondering where Aoife would have gone. Finally, I took a risk and stepped onto the main road, and saw a mountain of gold in the distance. I blinked and looked again, and realize it was a castle, but not like one of the stone castles that were so common in Clare. This was a shining gold and ivory structure that gleamed like a second sun.

Christ, Aoife had grown up surrounded by gold. What in the world did she see in my humble old farm?

I reached into my pocket, and touched the scrap of chain mail. Love, that's what she had at my farm, and with me.

I retreated back to the shadows, and skulked toward the palace. The closer I got the faster my heart beat; how would I gain entry to such a place, and how would I evade what had to be dozens or hundreds of guards? As I wondered if I was actually heading toward my death, a woman stepped in front of me.

"Are you Brian from the surface world?" she demanded.

"I am. Who's asking?"

"I'm Talia. Aoife's told me all about you." She turned, and beckoned for me to follow her. "Come along. I'll get you inside the palace."

THE FEAST

Swathed in deep green silk and crowned in gold, I entered the palace's feasting hall. All heads turned toward me, and as the crowd murmured I suppressed a smile. I'd always loved making an entrance.

"Aoife," boomed the king's voice. I turned toward the throne, and saw him, Steinar the Immoveable, my lord and father. "Come sit beside me, daughter."

I gathered my skirts and strode across the room and onto the dais, then I curtsied low. "Father."

He gestured to the empty throne beside him that my mother occasionally used. Since she wasn't present, I sat beside him.

"Lovely of you to join us," he said.

"You know how I enjoy a good feast." I scanned the crowd, but I didn't see Seamus or Corentin. That was unfortunate, since I liked to keep my enemies close.

"Where have you been?"

"Doing my best to keep the city safe, in accordance with the oath I swore," I replied. "How is King Gradlon?"

"He has returned to Ker Ys," he replied. "Shortly after you disappeared a woman arrived at his palace and left a set of twins behind. Apparently, she's claiming they're his." Father glanced at me, and added, "It seems you're no longer the most scandalous among us."

I swallowed my retort, and asked, "Does that mean his brother's no longer his heir?"

"What you really mean is, does that mean you're no longer betrothed to Corentin?" Father countered.

"It doesn't matter if I'm betrothed or not, since I won't be marrying him." When Father pursed his lips, I continued, "I would like to speak to you about that."

Father nodded. "Speak we shall, but after the feast."

"As you wish," I said. "What are we celebrating?" I asked, then Corentin strode onto the dais.

"We're celebrating the foolish plan to keep Kilstiffen aloft permanently." Corentin gestured to a servant, and a chair was set beside my father. Even worse, Corentin sat in it. "Aoife, it is a true pleasure to see you again. I trust you've been well?"

"Yes," I grumbled, then I turned to the king. "Father, this is madness. Kilstiffen cannot remain above without suffering repercussions from the surface dwellers."

"Let them come," Father said. "We can more than meet them."

I considered the many types of weaponry common above ground, and knew Father was wrong. "Father. Papa. They have massive flying boats that can drop bombs onto the city from the air, and hundreds of other types of missiles. If they determine we're a threat to them, they could destroy us!"

"What's more, if Kilstiffen remains aloft how long until Ker Ys is also known to the surface?" Corentin asked. "Or Evonium, or Kitezh? If all the portals rise up and remain open, those below will not be pleased."

"What of Oscar, and Mama?" I added, since my mother and brother resided below the city in Tir na nÓg. "What will this madness—"

"Enough," Father boomed. "We will speak. Later."

I had plenty more to say, but Father was right. This wasn't the sort of discussion to be had whilst sitting on a dais during a feast. Perhaps that was why he didn't say another word until the initial ceremonies were complete, and he, Corentin, and myself descended to our own table at the head of the room.

"Is that where you've been all this time?" Father asked. "The surface?"

"I've seen a bit of the land," I replied.

"You've been to the surface?" Corentin asked. His enthusiasm would have been wonderful in a puppy. In a prince, not so much. "What's it like?"

"Sunny," I replied, then I said to my father, "Those above have already noticed the city. What will happen when they decide to sail over for a cup of tea?"

"Our navy is strong," Father replied. "We will be safe. I will, however, accept a diplomatic envoy."

"Have you been to the surface often?" Corentin asked.

"We've all been above," I began, then he shook his head.

"I haven't," Corentin said. "Gradlon says it's a land of lawlessness and depravity. That's why our cities went below, in order to preserve a more pious way of life."

"Pious?" I repeated. "Exactly what is pious about your brother hauling off above and getting a few wee ones dropped on his doorstep?"

"We don't know if the twins are his," Corentin said, with a nod toward the pearl I wore at my throat. It had been a gift from my grandsire, Manannán mac Lir. "And their mother is a sea goddess's daughter, much like you are. Their bloodline will only strengthen ours."

I watched as Corentin's hand moved toward mine, and realized that when he said the word "ours" he meant me and him. "I've enough godly blood, thank you very much," I said as I folded my hands in my lap. "But honestly, Father, what do you really think will come of this?"

He blew out a breath, and transformed from the mighty king of Kilstiffen and into a tired old man. "Truly, Aoife, I wish you had been here with me these last few months. Seamus has won the council over, and I fear this plan will move forward no matter what I say."

"Who cares what the council thinks? You're the king. Only you can turn the golden key." Father nodded, but didn't meet my gaze. I lowered my voice, and said, "I'm sorry I was gone for so long. I was mad, but then something happened, and I needed someplace quiet to recuperate."

"Recuperate?" Father's head snapped up, his voice sharp. "Were you injured?"

"I was," I replied, then I told him exactly what had happened when I confronted Seamus in the council chamber. By the time I was finished Father's face was red as an apple and his fists were clenched like boulders.

"Setting his men on you, the heiress of Kilstiffen, is nothing short of treason," Father seethed. "I am putting a stop to his plans, and I'm doing it now."

"We'll do it together," I said, as I rose. "Let me change out of this gown and into my gear. I'll meet you at the council chamber."

"Aye, daughter," Father said. "Together we shall teach Seamus a lesson."

With that, Father and I stood, and went off in separate directions. He went to assemble the council and raise the guard, and I headed toward to my rooms to remove this too-tight gown. Corentin—whom I'd quite forgotten about—chose to follow me.

"I'm so glad you've returned to help the king see reason," he said, as he followed me down the corridor. "Steinar's been lost without you these past months."

"Has he?" I felt my heart clench; what with Scáthach overseeing her academy in Evonium and both Mama and Oscar residing below for now, I was the only family Father had left in Kilstiffen, and I'd abandoned him. "I didn't leave to make things difficult for him. Everything I said was true."

"I've no doubt," Corentin said. "You said your shoulder was injured in your altercation with Seamus?"

"Yes. One of Seamus's guards cracked me but good." We reached my door, and I paused to withdraw the key from the pouch on my belt. I always kept my rooms locked, and the only other key to my door in existence was possessed by Talia. "It took some time for the bruising to clear up," I continued, as I opened the door and pushed it open... and saw Brian standing in my bedchamber.

Gods below, how had he gotten into the palace?

"Brian," I began, then I felt Corentin's hand on my shoulder.

"Get off me!" I flicked his hand away as if he was a spider.

"Aoife, I just want to know if you're all right," Corentin murmured, as he replaced his hand on my shoulder. "I must look after my wife."

"Stop touching me, and don't ever call me that again!" I said, then Brian charged out of my door and punched Corentin square in the nose.

THE MOST WONDERFUL TRUTH

I probably shouldn't have clobbered the boy as hard as I did, but I didn't regret it. He was old enough to know better than to touch a woman without her permission. Aoife, however, was on track to have kittens.

"Gods below, why did you hit him?" she demanded. I opened my mouth to answer her, but nothing came out. Instead of the armour and boots she'd been wearing earlier, Aoife was clad in an amazing green gown that left one of her shoulders bare, golden shoes, and a tiara that resembled gilded coral. Add to that her usual gold bracelets and pearl pendant, and she looked like the queen of the sea.

Irritated by my speechlessness, she muttered, "Help me drag him inside."

"Don't you dare lift anything," Talia said, as she ushered Aoife inside the chamber. "Now Brian, we'll each take a leg and give him a good yank." I did as I was told, and we dragged the boy inside and shut the door. His head lolled to the side, and blood leaked from his nose.

"You got him good," Talia said, as she crouched beside him. "Brian, are you going to answer Aoife's question?"

"He was touching you, and he had no business doing it," I said. Aoife frowned, and wrung her hands. "I only wanted him to leave you be."

"You accomplished that," Aoife said. "Brian, mo ghrá, how did you come to be here?"

I withdrew the scrap of chain mail I found in the cave. "I followed you into the cave, and found this. I thought you'd been hurt, and you needed me."

Aoife looked at the mail sitting on my palm, then she wrapped her arms around me and pressed her cheek against my chest, right over my heart. "You came to rescue me?"

"I did, not that you need any rescuing." I tilted up her chin. "Are you all right?"

"I am now," she said. "I'm so glad you're here... But how are you here, inside the palace?"

"Talia found me, and brought me inside."

"You weren't that hard to find," Talia said. "I saw him from the balcony, skulking about the palace walls. Since he's dressed like a surface dweller, and you've been spending time above, I went to investigate."

Aoife laughed. "So much for Kilstiffen's legendary guard." She glanced at the man on the floor. "Will he be all right?"

"I think so," Talia replied. "Though I don't know how we'll avoid a diplomatic incident."

I grunted. "That mean he's Corentin?"

"He is, and we can say I hit him myself," Aoife replied. "He was the one laying hands on me, which he has no right to do."

"Still, we should get him up off the floor," Talia said. When Aoife moved to help her, Talia said, "I told you, no lifting."

"Why can't you lift anything?" I asked. Aoife was strong, and could probably carry this Corentin by herself. "Is your shoulder bothering you again?"

"No, not my shoulder." Aoife took my hand, and said, "Brian, I have the most wonderful news." Before she could continue her door banged open and an older man strode into the chamber. He took one look at Aoife and me holding hands, then at Corentin on the floor, and scowled.

"What is happening here?" he demanded, in a layered voice that told me he was a merrow like Aoife. "Who is this interloper? Did he attack the prince? Talia, call the guards!"

"Father, wait," Aoife said, as I winced. This I not how I had planned to meet her father. "You asked me if I've been above these past months, and the answer is yes. This is Brian Murphy, and I was with him."

"Were you?" Aoife's father said as he looked me over. The king was a tall, barrel chested man, and I understood why he was called Steinar the Immoveable. Nothing short of a crane could budge this fellow. "Why is Corentin bleeding on the floor?"

"He was struck in the face," Talia replied, in a rushed manner that told me Steinar's magic was at work. "By Brian."

"Was he?" Steinar demanded, then he faced me. "Why did you attack Prince Corentin?"

"He—" Aoife began.

"I asked the surface dweller," Steinar boomed.

"Corentin had his hand on Aoife's shoulder, and she told him to get off but he wouldn't listen," I said. "I do regret hitting him as hard as I did."

"Do you." Steinar turned to Aoife's maid, and ordered, "Talia, please fetch a healer." Talia curtsied, and left the room. "Now you can both explain how a surface dweller found his way into my city, and into my daughter's room."

"Aoife returned because she knew something was amiss with your city," I replied. "I followed her, because I thought she needed me."

Steinar scoffed. "Aoife is our greatest warrior. She needs no assistance from you or anyone."

"You're wrong, Papa," Aoife said, as she took my hand in both of hers. "I do need Brian. And we're having a baby."

I took a step back. "What?"

"It's why all my clothes are so tight," she said, as she set her hands on my shoulders. "I had no idea, not until Talia pointed it out. But it's true, and it's the most wonderful truth." When all I did was stare at her—for she'd rendered me speechless yet again—Aoife bit her lip. "Isn't it?"

"Aye," I said, having found my voice at last. "It is the best truth I have ever heard."

THE KING'S BLESSING

"You disappear for four months, return during the largest feast we've held since my coronation and cause a disruption, and now you're with child?" Father shook his head. "I should have sent you below instead of Oscar."

"Surely you don't mean that," I said.

"A crown prince has been assaulted, which is near to what earned Oscar his banishment," Father added.

"Oscar went after a set of dukes, not a prince," I pointed out. "And Corentin was laying hands on your pregnant daughter! Was Brian not in the right to defend me?"

Father grunted, then he held out his arms. I went to him, knowing I'd won him over. Not that it was ever very hard to sway Father to my side. "Aoife, Aoife. What am I to do with you?"

"You could begin by issuing a decree ending this farce of a betrothal," I suggested. "That would be a most excellent wedding gift for me and Brian, don't you think?"

"I suppose it must be formally ended." Father released me, looked at Corentin where he lay on the floor, and grimaced. "Tell me, did you find a suitor for the sole purpose of making yourself unavailable to him?"

"I was never available to that one," I said. "Brian, please tell Papa how you found me."

"I heard her singing," Brian said. "I was out on my boat, alone, when I heard the most beautiful sound. I followed it, and it led me straight to Aoife."

"Her heart called to you," Father said.

"Aye, sir, thought I can't say if her heart called to me, or if that song stole my own heart," Brian said. "I have been hopelessly in love with your daughter ever since."

"Isn't that how you met Mama?" I asked. "Didn't she hear you across the water?"

"She did," Father said, then he eyed Brian. "She was also from a different world."

Brian shrugged. "We cannot choose who we love, now can we?"

"No, we certainly cannot." Father spared a last glance for Corentin. "Come along, both of you. We're already in the midst of a feast. Now it will be your betrothal banquet."

"What of that one?" I asked, since I did not want Corentin lying about my chambers as if he belonged there.

"Lying on the cold floor in a pool of his own blood is a fitting punishment, don't you think?" Father countered. "Once the healers are done with him, I'll send him off with a letter detailing how he assaulted my pregnant daughter. That ought to put Gradlon in his place."

I laughed, and extended my hands to Brian. "I can't wait to show you my home."

THE REST OF THEIR DAYS

While I'd been all for the idea of a celebration, I hadn't realised the next order of business would be dressing me up like an undersea prince.

"You look wonderful," Aoife assured me, as she straightened my collar. Talia had secured a charcoal grey suit and ivory shirt for me that made me resemble a character from a Dickens novel. "Although you're most handsome without any clothes at all."

"Aoife," I admonished, my gaze darting about. "The last thing I need is for your father to overhear such a comment."

As always, Aoife shrugged it off. "Since I am carrying your child, he's most likely deduced I've seen you naked."

"There's another word he shouldn't be hearing."

"Brian. Don't be such a prude."

I shook my head. It was plain that Steinar the Immoveable was wrapped around his daughter's finger. "All right, my beauty. Are we ready to celebrate?"

She offered me her arm. "I'd say we are, mo ghrá."

When we reached the main hall, the celebration was already well underway. The city rising to the ocean's surface was usually a joyous time, understandably so. However, Steinar had just announced that they would be retreating beneath the waves at the next sunrise, instead of remaining an island as previously announced. I'd expected the residents to be disappointed, but they appeared as joyous as they had been before the announcement.

"How did everyone take the news?" Aoife asked the king, as we took our places at his table.

"Surprisingly well," Steinar replied. "As you know, we haven't been aloft for two consecutive days in centuries. Everyone seems to have had enough sun, for now."

Aoife smiled at her father, then she gave me a knowing glance. What had actually changed the populace's opinion of remaining on the surface were a few aircraft that flew overhead, and a rather large ship that got a bit too close to the shore. Those of Kilstiffen now appreciated how safe they were beneath the waves, far away from so-called modern terrors.

Steinar stood, and waited for the crowd's attention. "My people, our fortune knows no bounds, for we now have a second reason to celebrate. My youngest child, Aoife, the champion of Kilstiffen, is to be married!"

The room erupted in cheers, as Aoife blushed and waved at the well-wishers. After a bit of coaxing we stood, and the cheers increased to a roar. I was certain they could hear us all the way in Doolin.

"Your people love you, my beauty," I said. "But not as much as I do."

After our meal, Aoife and Steinar took me around the palace. It was a glorious place, with nearly every surface adorned with gold and pearls and other precious items. When I thought it couldn't possibly get more decadent, then took me to a small room clad entirely in gold.

"This is where we turn the key," Steinar explained, then he reached into a mechanism and gave it a good crank. "The key is what allows us to rise and fall, so we may keep those above and below safe. Ours is a sacred duty, Brian."

"Yes, sir." I was having a hard time figuring out how to refer to the king. Technically he would be my father-in-law, but I suspected calling him Da was out of the question. "Do you keep the key on your person, for safety?"

"Once, I did. Now, I secure it in my rooms." Steinar saw a gathering at the far end of the corridor, and frowned. "Excuse me."

"I wonder what that's about," Aoife murmured, then she gasped. "Turn around. MacCreehy's at the end of the hall, surrounded by guards. They're probably hauling him off to the prison caves."

"Is he?" I craned my neck to get a look at the man who'd caused my beauty such strife. Aoife pulled me around a corner, out of the man's view.

"I don't want him to see you," she said. "If he sees you, he can find you. We need to start our life fresh, and not be constantly looking over our shoulders for that villain." She laced her fingers with mine. "All I want, Brian Murphy, is to spend the rest of my days with you."

I wrapped my arms around my soon to be wife, and kissed her forehead. "That, my beauty, is the best idea I've ever heard."

Now you know how the fisherman rescued the mermaid. If you're new to the world of Merrowkin, turn the page for a sneak peek from the first book in the series.

MERROWKIN CHAPTER ONE: THE CLIFFS

"*Daddy, do I look like my mommy?*"
    "*Aye, that you do, Meri girl.*"
"*Where did she go? Why doesn't she want to live with us anymore?*"
"*She needed to return to the sea.*"

I burst into the kitchen and tripped over the threshold, but managed to catch the edge of the table before I hit the floor. I wasn't usually so clumsy, but this wasn't an ordinary Monday. For the first time, I was going on the school field trip to the Cliffs of Moher. Also of note, I was defying my father for the first time in my life.

The kettle whistled as I carefully forged my father's name on the permission slip. It wasn't perfect, but it was passable. My hands shook as I poured the water, but I made my tea without scalding myself. That done, I got the bread that I'd set out to rise the night before into the oven, and took stock of the larder. We had fish, fish, and more fish. Yum. That, coupled with the bread, meant Kevin and I would eat today, and perhaps again tomorrow, but the day after that was looking a bit uncertain. It was Kevin's turn to do the shopping, and his version of a balanced meal was a bag of crisps with a glass of milk. And for the love of all that is holy, couldn't he bring home a vegetable for once, or maybe some fruit? It would be terrible to expire due to scurvy, what with us living in the twenty-first century and all.

I also noticed two bottles of whiskey standing at attention on top of the refrigerator, one more than usual. Interesting.

I jotted a few items on a list and taped it to Kevin's bedroom door. Hopefully, he would notice it when he woke. Shopping list sorted, I sought out lunch money. Being that Da had already left for his fishing boat I went to the tall hutch in the dining room and opened the drawer on the left.

There were two envelopes in the drawer, and in those envelopes was where Da left our allowances. On one of them was written *Meri girl*, and on the other *Kevin lad*, both in Da's messy scrawl. I have never opened Kevin's envelope, and I trust that he's never opened mine. Even siblings need privacy now and then. *Especially* siblings.

I pocketed the euros, and by the time I'd got myself showered, the bread had baked up nicely. I set it aside to cool while I dressed, then I took a big slice and left for my classes at Saint Senan and Saint Conainne's Academy. That name was a mouthful, so we students called it The Saints.

School was... Well, it was there. I've never been one of those studious sorts, the ones who lived and died depending on their marks. I was a good enough student, and my grades reflected that, but the classes were just so boring. Once I was taught a bit of science or mathematics and understood how the concept worked, I lost all interest in the subject. And don't get me started on the atrocious reading material my literature teachers assigned with grim enthusiasm. I don't care if James Joyce was a national treasure, *Finnegan's Wake* is nigh on unintelligible.

Beyond the boring classes, the worst part about school was that everyone knew me as the mermaid's daughter, and that was no one's fault but my own. When my mother had left us all those years ago, I was inconsolable. I'd only been three years old, and I could not understand where Mama was or why no one would tell me when she was coming home. Da, in his kindest, most foolish moment, told me that my mother was in reality a mermaid, and had returned to her people under the sea.

At that, my tears had given way to a proud smile. My Mama was an important mermaid, of course she couldn't be mucking around up here on land. There was work—important work—to do down below, and she'd return to us soon enough.

I don't know if Da had expected me to believe him, or if he'd told me that story the way other parents warn their children to be wary of fairy circles and black cats crossing their path. But believe him I did, and when I started school, I told all my classmates about my beautiful mermaid mother. In hindsight, that had not been a very good idea. Somehow, I endured the resultant name-calling and teasing into my fifth year, though I'd considered leaving school many times. I didn't want to live as an uneducated minor, so a student I stayed.

Relentless teasing aside, the only subject that had ever interested me at school was music. I loved singing, and whenever I sang, the world fell away as I lost myself in the ebb and flow of the notes. Even though I was one of the strongest voices in the choir, I kept to the chorus. Standing in the front of the pack with the entire auditorium staring at me was quite a bit more attention than I could handle. What with all the backhanded comments regularly tossed my way—*Meri's got a voice like her mum, have a care or her siren's song will make us follow her to our doom*—I didn't need the added scrutiny.

Let me tell you, if I could have controlled that lot with a song, I would never have them follow me like a modern day Pied Piper. Sending them off in the opposite direction, now that would be a fine trick.

When I arrived at school, I was greeted by the mad chaos that was a hundred or so students being herded onto buses for our day trip to the Cliffs. The weather was grey and cold, but that hadn't dampened anyone's enthusiasm. It was a day out of school, after all. I saw which bus Aodhan was queued up near, turned on my heel and went to the farthest one from him.

It's not that I didn't like Aodhan. I did, very much so, and I'd spent countless hours wondering if his hair felt as soft and silky as it looked. But I was only seventeen, and the last thing I needed was to be someone's girlfriend. I needed to figure out for myself who Meri Murphy was before I could go around sharing her with others.

After I handed off my forged permission slip, I boarded the bus and scored a window seat. As I stared out the window, I wondered if Da was aware of this trip, and if that was why he'd stockpiled the extra bottle of whiskey at home. No matter why he'd got the booze, I refused to stay behind—again—while the rest of my class got to visit one of the greatest sights in Ireland. This time, I wouldn't be left behind, and I'd see for myself the place where my parents had met all those years ago.

I could use a drop of whiskey myself.

A wadded-up ball of paper hit my head and bounced onto my lap. Behind me, I could hear Kelsey McGrath and Sarah Haynes snickering. They'd been the architects of my troubles for as long as I could remember, though to my knowledge I'd never done anything to either of them. I smoothed the paper out against the back of the seat in front of me to learn what today's torment entailed. It was a rather nice sketch of a mermaid, bare breasts and all.

My face went hot and my hands trembled. Even after years of being teased, a simple sketch could still reduce me to a weepy, snotty mess. I bit the inside of my mouth and got myself under control, then I tilted my head back and yelled, "It's a lovely likeness. Thank you for your consideration."

There was a great deal of laughter toward the back of the bus. The school's headmaster, Seamus MacCreehy, got up from his seat to investigate. "What's all the yelling about?" he demanded.

"Nothing, sir," I said in a rush. MacCreehy was an absolute terror, on account of his loud rumble of a voice and his tall, broad frame, which was better suited to a rugby player than a professional educator.

His eyes narrowed. "You're certain it's nothing?"

"I am." I hadn't made the mistake of attempting to seek justice against those bullies since I was ten. "Someone drew a picture of a mermaid and tossed it up to me. It's really quite good."

I handed over the wrinkled paper. His brow creased when he saw the sketch. "Times past we called them merrows."

"What was that, sir?"

"Mermaids. We once called them merrows, and their children the merrowkin." Mr MacCreehy blinked and refocused on me. I could see his inner battle waging; should he reprimand whomever had sketched the mermaid, or just let it go? Eventually, he jerked his head toward the back of the bus and asked, "Has that lot been bothering you, Meredith?"

Ugh. I hated my given name. "Not at all," I said with a smile. "Just a bit of fun."

He grunted, then he stuffed the paper in his back pocket and returned to his seat. Just as I was congratulating myself on that small victory, Aodhan Sullivan slid into the seat beside me.

"Hey, Meri," he said. "What's the what?"

Aodhan was as much of an outlier at school as I was, though for different reasons. His father was not only black, but American to boot. The elder Sullivan had been some kind of surfing celebrity in California, and after winning all the trophies and setting several world records, he'd relocated to western Ireland and opened a surf shop. The school lasses all followed Aodhan like lovesick puppies, describing him as worldly and cultured compared to the rest of the boys. Never mind that Aodhan had been born right here in County Clare, and was therefore about as exotic as a goat.

If I cared about such things as boys I'd say he was a handsome one, tall and lean with dark hair and wide brown eyes. But I don't care about those things, so to me he's just regular old Aodhan.

"Is this seat taken?" he asked, when I only stared at him in silence.

"I saw you getting on a different bus," I blurted out.

"I was, then I saw you get on this one and I switched. What was that about?" he asked, jerking his chin toward Mr MacCreehy.

"Same old," I replied. "Someone thought it would be smart to bonk me in the head with a picture of a mermaid."

"Sullivan," MacCreehy yelled. "Quit bothering Meredith and find a different seat."

"Can't, sir. The rest have all been claimed." Aodhan gestured behind him, indicating the full bus. MacCreehy opened his mouth, but the driver shut the door and announced that we were pulling away from the school, and could everyone please sit down and buckle up? After shooting a final warning glare at Aodhan, MacCreehy returned to his seat.

"Wasn't that a bit of excitement," Aodhan said, then he tipped his head toward the back of the bus. "Why do you let them act that way? Really, Meri, you need to stand up for yourself."

"If I do, they'll just find some other way to harass me."

"But, Meri—"

"I don't want to talk about it." I turned my face toward the window, because damn it all I was not going to cry on a bus to a school field trip after getting bonked in the head with a drawing of a mermaid. I do have some dignity left.

I felt a soft warmth on my fingers. I looked down; Aodhan had placed his hand on mine. Any other time I would have shooed him away, but right then I needed a friend. I curled my little finger around his, but didn't acknowledge him in any other way. He smiled, and we rode in silence to the Cliffs.

Less than an hour later, our caravan of buses pulled into the car park at the Cliffs of Moher. Once they were properly arranged, we disembarked, crossed the road to the Visitor Centre, and got ourselves sorted out. The centre itself was built right into the hillside, and it sat quite near to the cliff's edge. The whole effect made me feel like we'd reached the end of the world. Surely we'd reached the end of Ireland proper.

Since there were four busloads of students, we were organised accordingly into four tour groups. That meant that I was in the group with those who found it amusing to pick on my unfortunate family situation. It also meant that I was in the group with Aodhan. His presence made the rest a bit more bearable.

"Have you ever been here before?" Aodhan asked.

"I think once, when I was small." I didn't add that any trips I'd made to the sea would have taken place back when Mama was still with us. Ever since she'd left, Da hated the very notion of Kevin and I possibly following her into the waves, even though he's out on his boat every day, trawling for fish and guzzling whiskey. It's a wonder he hasn't drowned.

Luckily, Da was still with us, but despite the way he chooses to spend his days, he has forbidden both Kevin and I from ever approaching the sea. A challenging thing to do when you live on an island, yes, but being that I hate the idea of swimming, it's not too difficult for me to avoid the beach.

"Meri!"

"What?" I turned away from the water and stared at Aodhan.

"Have you heard a word I said?" he demanded.

"I was looking at the waves. What were you saying?"

"Are you excited to see the Cliffs?"

"I guess I am excited," I said.

Aodhan's grin returned. "Me, too."

I turned back toward the sea. "My parents met here."

Aodhan's brows rose. "They met at the Visitor Centre?"

"No, at a beach down below. Da was out on his boat and Mama was stranded. He rescued her."

"Huh. I guess that's where the mermaid bit came from."

I swallowed the lump in my throat. "I guess so. Let's queue up with the rest."

It was a windy day, but I guessed it always was there on account of the Cliffs' amazing height. If I remembered correctly, we were about two hundred metres above sea level, and it was a sheer drop straight down to the water. While the school administrators and park officials were deciding which group of students should take the nature walk first, I turned toward the ocean.

Even though I couldn't see the waves crashing against the shore, I could hear them mercilessly beating the rocks. An island sat atop the waves, so small it was like a pebble lying on a vast blue rug. At first, I assumed it was one of the Aran Isles, but then a bit of gold flashed on the ocean's surface.

I closed my eyes and shook my head. It had to have been a trick of the light, or perhaps it was due to me being unaccustomed to the great height. Any gold would have to be the reflection of the sun on the water, though since the day was overcast, I didn't know how that could be. I opened my eyes and looked again; yes, there was the gold, surrounding the island and scattered across the top. If I craned my neck just so I could make out a roof—no, make that a cluster of roofs—and what looked like a church's spire...

Shouts from behind roused me. I looked down, and saw nothing but the sea crashing against the rocks. Just like mama had done, I was going home.

Need to know what happens next? Continue the story here: https://books2read.com/Merrowkin

ALSO BY JENNIFER ALLIS PROVOST

The Order of the Phoenix
The Phoenix and the Cat
Phoenix Rising
Dragon Descending

The Chronicles of Parthalan, a six volume epic fantasy (and one short story collection)
Heir to the Sun
The Virgin Queen
Rise of the Deva'shi
Pieces of Parthalan: Six All-New Stories From The Land of Parthalan
Golem
Elfsong
Sunfall

The Copper Legacy, a four book urban fantasy:
Copper Girl
Copper Ravens
Copper Veins
Copper Princess

A duology based in the Copper world:
Redemption
Salvation

Poison Garden, an urban fantasy filled with seers, witches, and one seriously hot detective:
Belladonna
Oleander
Bleeding Hearts
Thornapple
Wolfsbane
Mistletoe
Mandrake

Gallowglass, an urban fantasy set in Scotland and New York:
Gallowglass
Walker
Homecoming
The Shades of Elphame

Winter's Queen, an urban fantasy set in Scotland and Elphame:
Touch of Frost
Giant's Daughter
Elphame's Queen

Merrowkin, an urban fantasy set in Ireland above and below
Merrowkin
Death's Door
Manannán's Pearl
A Sea of Secrets and Salvation

Changes, a contemporary romance:

Changing Teams
Changing Scenes
Changing Fate
Changing Dates

ABOUT THE AUTHOR

Jennifer Allis Provost is a native New Englander who lives in a sprawling colonial along with her beautiful and precocious twins, a dog that thinks she's a kangaroo, a parrot, a junkyard cat, and a wonderful husband who never forgets to buy ice cream. As a child, she read anything and everything she could get her hands on, including a set of encyclopedias, but fantasy was always her favorite. She spends her days drinking vast amounts of coffee, arguing with her computer, and avoiding any and all domestic behavior.

Find Jenn on the web here: http://authorjenniferallisprovost.com/

For up to the minute sale notifications, follow her on Bookbub here: https://www.bookbub.com/profile/jennifer-allis-provost
    For exclusive content, follow her on Patreon: https://www.patreon.com/jenniferallisprovost/
    Friend her on Facebook: http://www.facebook.com/jennallis
    Follow her on Instagram: @jenniferaprovost
    Happy reading!

www.ingramcontent.com/pod-product-compliance
Lightning Source LLC
LaVergne TN
LVHW041710060526
838201LV00043B/668